34516

M   Stein, Aaron Marc

A nose for it.

34516

M   Stein, Aaron Marc

A nose for it.

DATE	ISSUED TO
NOV 6 1980	Cosentino
NOV 1 3 1980	C. JARRETT
DEC 6 1980	Lee Wayne
DEC 1 5 1980	

A Nose for It

By Aaron Marc Stein

A NOSE FOR IT
THE CHEATING BUTCHER
ONE DIP DEAD
THE ROLLING HEADS
NOWHERE?
BODY SEARCH
LEND ME YOUR EARS
COFFIN COUNTRY
LOCK AND KEY
THE FINGER
ALP MURDER
KILL IS A FOUR-LETTER
  WORD
SNARE ANDALUCIAN
DEADLY DELIGHT
I FEAR THE GREEKS
BLOOD ON THE STARS
HOME AND MURDER
NEVER NEED AN ENEMY
SITTING UP DEAD
MOONMILK AND MURDER
DEATH MEETS 400 RABBITS

THE DEAD THING IN THE
  POOL
MASK FOR MURDER
PISTOLS FOR TWO
SHOOT ME DACENT
FRIGHTENED AMAZON
THREE—WITH BLOOD
THE SECOND BURIAL
DAYS OF MISFORTUNE
THE CRADLE AND THE
  GRAVE
WE SAW HIM DIE
DEATH TAKES A PAYING
  GUEST
. . . AND HIGH WATER
THE CASE OF THE ABSENT-
  MINDED PROFESSOR
ONLY THE GUILTY
THE SUN IS A WITNESS
HER BODY SPEAKS
SPIRALS

A Nose for It

AARON MARC STEIN

PUBLISHED FOR THE CRIME CLUB BY

DOUBLEDAY & COMPANY, INC.

GARDEN CITY, NEW YORK

1980

All of the characters in this book
are fictitious, and any resemblance
to actual persons, living or dead,
is purely coincidental.

ISBN: 0-385-17189-7
Library of Congress Catalog Card Number 80–947
Copyright © 1980 by Aaron Marc Stein
All Rights Reserved
Printed in the United States of America
First Edition

For
My friends the Offneckers
of
the Backshore Road.

A Nose for It

CHAPTER 1

There was a time when it had been bloody ground. That spit of land stretching out toward the Atlantic had in its day had more than its share of killing. All that, however, seemed to be safely in the past. The town had gotten it over with early in its history, back in the days of those seventeenth-century wranglings we call the French and Indian Wars.

Back in those days it was a little wilderness outpost. Every time it was attacked it fell, and it went through repeated wipeouts when the Indians would swoop down and massacre everybody. If you wander around the town, you'll hit a historical marker at every turn and I know of no place where the markers drip more gore. Once it was successfully defended when a force from Massachusetts came up to secure it for the Revolution and the British garrison beat them off. In 1812 it reverted to its old ways and fell to the British, but that had been the last of it. Any violence committed since had been inflicted only on lobsters, fish, clams, crabs, and scallops. Man was at peace.

I was there to help a man die. It might be better said that I was there to help a man live through such little time as he had left to him. Without placing any blame, I can say it was because of him that I made what for me was a radically uncharacteristic move. That move put me up to my eyes in murder.

The man was General Sam Dalton. Back when I first
knew him he was Colonel Dalton, but then I was the
youngest and craziest captain in his command. Before the
war was over and he had made Brigadier, I had still not
yet begun to make sense. Then the war was over and the
army kept handing him additional stars. I made civilian
and went back to school before he made Major General.
That came to him along about the time that I maybe
made adult. In the course of the war there had been
many colonels in my life but Dalton was the only one of
them worth remembering. For some reason, he for his
part thought me worth remembering, so we never fell out
of touch. To say that we were friends would be true
enough but for one omitted dimension. There was something of a father-and-son feeling to our relationship.

Whenever time and geography permitted, I would stop
by to touch base with him and, after he retired and settled into the old house on Penobscot Bay, it became one
of my regular ports of call. We'd sail together and golf together and fish together. For far more years than you will
believe, we also had tennis. The old boy was inde-
structible. It was hard to recognize that he wouldn't be
going on forever.

But nobody does. The time came when I called him
and I got Millie. Millie was his granddaughter. When I'd
first known her, she hadn't yet cut her first tooth. To me
that might have seemed like only yesterday, but to Millie,
of course, it was a lifetime. We had gone through a spell
of years when she was too big a girl to sit on Uncle
Matt's knee anymore. When last I'd seen her, she had
taken to doing it again, but since she was twenty, it was
not what it had been.

"He's sick, Matt. He's awfully sick."

"What's wrong?" I asked.

"Just about everything."

"What's 'just about everything'?"

"The doctor says his kidneys, his liver, heart, everything."

We'd played tennis on his eightieth birthday and eight-year-old Millie had been ball girl. The arithmetic was easy. Sam Dalton was ninety-three. He'd earned the right to be falling apart. They were a long time getting him to the phone, but Millie told me to hang on. Sam insisted on doing it. He was determined to talk to me.

Even if she'd told me nothing, I would have known it as soon as he came on. There was nothing left of the old parade-ground bellow. It had withered down to a shallow-breathed wheeze. The words were what they had always been, but now they seemed unreal, as though they belonged to someone else.

I told him to get well for when I'd be coming up to see him.

"Not this year, my boy. We'll say good-by now. I made them bring me to the phone for that."

"No, Sam," I said. "I'm not nearly ready to say any good-by and not this way ever. I'm coming up."

"Against orders, Matt."

"I was always insubordinate. You can't think I'm going to change now."

"I've got this young fellow here. He helps me up. He puts me down. He wipes my chin. It's nothing you want to see."

"He won't be in our way, Sam. We'll give him some time off."

"And you'll wipe my chin? No, Matt."

"You're going to have to tell me. When did we stop being friends?"

It had come at a good time. You know who I am—

Matthew Erridge, engineer. I had some things going here
and there, but nothing that needed my presence, nothing
that I couldn't delegate. I was handling all the stuff by
telephone and I could do that from Maine as well as from
home in Morristown or the New York office. I threw a
couple of suitcases into the Porsche, let Mathilda seduce
me into taking her along, and hit the road. Mathilda is
my dog. She's a basset of most friendly disposition, and
ever since I've owned her, Sam Dalton has been one of
her special friends. She thought she could kiss him and
make him well. She has these delusions about those
sloppy kisses of hers.

It's a long drive from New Jersey up to Maine, and the
Penobscot area is a good piece beyond the New Hamp-
shire border. If I could have given the Porsche her head,
Baby would have made it much shorter, but there are
states up that way that get serious enough about the fifty-
five-mile-an-hour speed limit to make restraint the better
part of wisdom. Restraint was in the neighborhood of
seventy.

So it was evening before we hit the shores of the bay.
Sam had had his supper and he was sleeping. He woke
during the evening and we had a little time together.
Millie left us to it, but Dexter hung around.

I can't say I took to Dexter at first sight, but I can say
it took only a little time to move me from having no special feeling about him one way or the other to developing
an all but irresistible urge to kick his ass.

He was a big guy. He carried an impressive mass of
muscle. Guessing at his age, if you'll allow me a margin
of a year or two either way, I'll call it thirty. He was
good-looking but with an incongruous prettiness. His
good looks made him look fake. You couldn't believe all
of him and you didn't know which to believe—the pretty

face or the rugged body. There was something obscene about the look of him, like a guy in drag.

He carried a comb in his hip pocket and his hands were never idle. When he had nothing else to do with them, which seemed to be all too much of the time, he combed his hair. Even at the table between courses he would get in a few sweeps of the comb. He knew his job and it was evident that he handled it well. The helping up and putting down were no exaggeration. Sam was shaky and feeble. He needed helping and there were times when it was more than helping. It was almost nothing short of carrying.

Dexter had the strength for it and, having the strength, he was able to manage it gently and, as far as was possible, unobtrusively. There was never any puffing or panting or straining. If he would only have kept his fool mouth shut, he could have been ideal for the nurse-companion job, but he would never shut up and there was nothing that came out of his mouth that wasn't wrong. He talked about Sam as though Sam wasn't there or was deaf or was too stupefied with senility to understand. In speaking to him, he didn't use baby talk, but he came close. It was the indulgent, condescending tone.

It did me good to see the way Sam handled it. He took it only till the first time Dexter tried to butt in on our talk. We were having none of that.

"Go someplace and look at yourself in the mirror for an hour or two," Sam said. "We'll let you know when I need you."

Dexter laughed and gave me a wink. He was taking it with the isn't-the-old-man-cute touch. I wasn't about to play that game. I snapped at him.

"You heard the general," I said.

"Think you can handle it?" Dexter asked.

"I can handle it."

"Call me if anything . . ."

"Just get lost," Sam said.

It was only that first evening. After that, more and more the man took to going off and leaving Sam with me. Those evenings were extra free time for him. I had been there a couple of days when Dexter's regular evening off came around. The way they had been handling it had been with Millie staying in to hold the fort during those times. There was this guy she was dating. He'd come to dinner and stay the evening, presumably to help out if Sam needed anything.

With Erridge there the guy wasn't going to be needed. Millie asked me if I wanted to go anywhere, and I thought maybe she wanted me out of the way.

"I'll be with Sam," I said.

"If you won't mind then, I'll go out," she said.

"Sure," I said. "We'll be okay, just the two of us."

The guy came around to pick her up. He looked better than Dexter, at least to the extent that he seemed to be all of a piece. He wasn't my sort of a guy. He was too smooth and too slick and for Millie I would have said he was by ten years or more too old. He didn't carry a comb in the hip pocket of his jeans, but I wasn't too much impressed by that. It could have been because on his forty-year-old skull he didn't have all that much hair.

His name was Creighton Douglas, a fancy man with a fancy name. He was driving a Jag. The way he handled it, he didn't deserve it. But he wasn't my date. He was Millie's and Uncle Matt was minding his own business. All the time we were eating, Sam talked of this and that, but it was evident that his mind wasn't more than half on what he was saying. Clara, the woman who came in by the day, was giving us dinner.

When we had finished and she had gone home, Sam switched to what he had on his mind.

"This Douglas fellow," he said. "Did you get to talk to him, Matt?"

"The few suitable words."

"What did you think of him?"

"He needs driving lessons."

"He needs more than that. He needs a kick in the ass."

"A couple of words, Sam. I didn't get to know him that well."

"If I was in better shape, I'd send Millie away."

"She's a big girl now. The time comes when you get over thinking for them and you let them make their own mistakes."

"There are boys around and they don't have wives. If she has to make mistakes, I'd rather she did it with one of them."

"He has a wife? Where is she?"

"Right here in town, but giving her time to another man, her time and what have you."

"The world moves on, Sam."

"It's moved right out from under me, Matt. I've lived too long."

He wasn't being sorry for himself. He was just giving me his estimate of the situation. He had tried to send Millie away. He had Dexter and Clara. Between them they took care of his physical needs. He'd been telling Millie that he was all right. He'd had his life and he shouldn't have been taking any of hers.

"For her own good I'd like her to be away from here. She won't leave."

"You think because of this Douglas jerk?"

"No, because of me. She's staying for my good. Of course, it isn't that I don't like having her around, but still. You know, that's what happens when you get old enough, Matt. In determining what's good for you, everybody knows better than you do yourself."

"You're afraid she'll get hurt? She's serious about this Douglas?"

"Serious? Not a chance. She's amusing herself with him, but that doesn't mean she can't get hurt."

"Not irreparably," I said. "If she's only amusing herself, she won't get badly hurt."

We didn't get much past that before Sam began nodding. I helped him to bed. The Sox were playing the Angels that night. Up in Maine you're in Red Sox country. I sat at the TV and watched the ball game. The Sox wrapped up a nice win, and I stayed with the tube for the eleven o'clock news. After that it was a movie. I watched that till the second commercial. I felt cathode poisoning begin to set in and I switched it off and fixed myself a drink. I took it to the window where I looked at the moonlight on the water and the lights of Belfast across the bay. Sam always had a taste for the right books. I picked one off the shelf and I read awhile. It got to be well after one and nobody had come home. Dexter evidently was stretching his evening off. It was beginning to look as though he was making a night of it. I wrote him a note and tacked it to the outside of Sam's bedroom door. I wasn't of a mind to sit up waiting for him, and I didn't want to be around when Douglas would bring Millie home. It could get her to thinking I'd been waiting up for her and that's not Erridge's style.

I let Mathilda out for a run and hung around only until she was ready to come back in. Then I went to bed. I took the cot in Sam's room. That was where Dexter slept, available in case Sam woke and wanted something. Dexter also had a room of his own, but that was for when someone was spelling him with Sam. Since I was taking over the duty for the rest of the night, I was telling Dexter as much in the note I'd tacked to the door.

The noise woke me and I think it must have been the first of it. I had, after all, been having that kind of sleep, ready to be up at the first sound from Sam, but with that kind of noise I probably would have wakened out of any kind of sleep. It came from the beach, out beyond the end of the garden.

It was the sound of revelry by night, laughing and shouting and hooting. I listened for some minutes and I looked at my watch. It was four-fifteen and I wondered about that. So it was an all-night party. They happen, but it seemed much too late for one to be just starting up, late even for one that had started at some more usual time and only now was reaching the noisy stage. Thinking about it that way, I concluded that it would have to be a movable feast. It had been going on somewhere else and then it had reached the place where it had seemed a good drunken idea to go skinny-dipping and it had there-fore transferred to the beach.

Since it didn't seem to be disturbing Sam, I reached into my slogan bag for that good old one—live and let live —and I turned over on my other ear. Of course, I was reckoning without Mathilda. It isn't that she isn't with me on the live-and-let-live business. It's just that she has her own way of reacting to noise. If there's any going, Mathilda has to have a part of it. People shout. People laugh. People cavort. Mathilda joins the fun. She barks. They are her happy barks, but those are her noisiest. She hauls them up out of her rear paws and resonates them through the full length of her long body. Give Mathilda the idea that it's happy time and she'll be deafening.

I knew her too well to kid myself that by ordering her

to shut up I might accomplish anything. Maybe they taught her something in obedience school, but there's no way of testing it out. After all, you can't expect her to respond to an order she can't hear past her own gargantuan woofs. Sam was having a good sleep, and Mathilda was a cinch for hauling him out of it. I jumped into pants and moccasins and rushed her out of the house.

The main idea was that I would put some distance between my inordinately noisy pup and Sam. Second thought had me taking her away in the direction of the beach. The loonies were down there. It was their untimely noise that was triggering Mathilda. Erridge was going to go to the root of the matter. Once I'd turned them off, I could work at turning Mathilda off as well. Peace and quiet could break out again.

You're not going to understand what came next unless I fill you in a bit on the local topography. The house looks out over the water. Through its west windows you have a tree-framed, unimpeded vista straight across to the far shore of the bay. It's great for looking at the water and for watching the seals at play on the offshore rocks. The stretch of rock-strewn beach that rims the near shore, however, is out of sight. Westward from the house there is a sizable stretch of garden and an even broader stretch of lawn.

All of this, though, sits atop a bluff. It's a low bluff, no towering palisade, just a rock-ribbed bit of the rock-ribbed coast of Maine, but it is high enough to drop out of view the narrow stretch of beach that lies at its foot.

There is a steep and tortuous path down the face of the bluff. If, on starting away from the house, I'd had any thought of going all the way down to the beach, I might have had the forethought to stop long enough on my way out to pick up a flashlight. I'd been down that path no few times over the years; but, nevertheless, it was nothing like home territory. Such memory as I might have had of it wasn't nearly enough for lightly undertaking to manage its treacheries in the dark.

I had figured on going only as far as that edge of the lawn where the rocks reared up through the grass and then dropped away to the beach. I could call down to the revelers from up there and we could parley at that distance. I was expecting it to be easy enough. All that noise they were making, however heedless or inconsiderate, was cheerful, good-humored noise. I could hear no aggression in it and no hostility.

I was going to ask no more of them than that they take it someplace else. They had picked a poor spot for their fun and games, just by a house where a sick old man was getting some hard-won sleep. I couldn't imagine that a few such words wouldn't be enough. If these guys happened to be locals, I would, of course, have more going for me. It had been a long retirement for the general. He'd had all those years when he had been getting around as good as ever. He had friends all over the place. He was a popular figure and now in his decline he wouldn't have been forgotten. I'd just mention his name and say he was sleeping.

It occurred to me that the probabilities were that they wouldn't be locals. Locals wouldn't need to be told. They would know that Sam lived there just above the beach and they would know he was old and sick. These might be summer renters or, even more likely, some crazy young bucks wandering the countryside in a hell-raising peregrination.

I was no more than halfway across the lawn with Mathilda galumphing along beside me in full cry when what had been good-natured hilarity suddenly became

something that was very much else. There was a shot,
only the one, and it was followed by sudden and complete silence.

I've been places where silly revelers, out of nothing
more than their love of noise, shoot off revolvers into the
air, but then it will never be a single shot and it will
never drop the whole caper into an ominous quiet. Mathilda is an intelligent dog. She read it just as I did. The
fun was over. She stopped barking and she pulled in close
to me. I could feel her rub her flank against my leg.

We went on to the end of the lawn. From the top of
the bluff I could look down onto the beach, but there
wasn't much I could see. It was a clear night. The whole
of the sky was glittering with stars, but the moon had set.
Stars, however much they might light up the sky, don't
give you any great deal down at ground level.

That close, from where I was right above it, there was
again something I could hear. Now, however, it was only
small and stealthy sounds. I could hear whispering. It
was only just loud enough to reach my ears. It wasn't giving me so much that I could make out any of the words.
There were some little clicks. Those would be kicked
pebbles. Looking down, I could see one light on the
beach. It was a flashlight, one of the big, powerful jobs. It
was lying on the beach and illuminating not much of
anything. It silhouetted some small stones and a dark
patch of irregular shape that looked like a black, tattered
rag. That would be seaweed, washed ashore and dried on
the beach.

I was feeling with my feet for the beginning of the
path that would take me down over the face of the bluff.
I was squeezing hard on my memory, trying to wring out
of it some remembrance of just where the path took off
from the lawn and how it went in its twisted course. I

found it and, with no little expectation that I was going to break a leg or two before I'd have followed it the whole of its length, I began feeling my way down it.

It was difficult to follow but by no means the impossibility I'd expected it would be. If I could have seen my way, I would have been down it in a matter of moments. In the dark, however, it was slow going. What made it possible was that, where it wasn't taking advantage of such natural rock gaps as offered, it had been cut in the rock. Sliding my feet to either side, I came up against the rocks that rimmed it. Guiding between them, I worked my way down.

All the way I was listening, working at picking up any small sound that wasn't Mathilda's or my own. Our progress wasn't nearly as quiet as I would have liked it to be. Feeling my way down, I kept dislodging some small, loose stones and, bouncing from rock to rock, they would go rolling down ahead of me.

So I wasn't hearing much of which I could be certain. I was still on the way down—how much of the way I had no way of knowing—when some louder sounds came up at me. Those I could be certain weren't of my own making. First it was some fairly loud splashing. That was nothing like the smaller sound of the water lapping against the shore. It was not only that it was louder. It was also out of rhythm. It was hurried and it was urgent. It had nothing of the placid laziness of cove water in a time of calm. It had to be the splash of hurried wading out from the shore.

It was followed by something even louder and that was immediately identifiable. It was the explosive roar of a small boat engine starting up. As it settled into its cruising rhythm, the noise of it throttled down and began a slow fade. It had taken off. It was putting a steadily widening distance between itself and the shore. The beach had gone almost totally quiet. Now there was nothing but the gentle lapping of the water against the rocks. The flashlight was still there, still lighting up the pebbles and the shreds of seaweed.

For following the path I couldn't guide on it. Twisting its way between rock outcroppings, the path took too many turns. That light, nevertheless, was good for one thing. I could use it for reading vertical distance. I was more than halfway down and I began to move along at a better clip. I was down far enough so that I could now risk a fall. There wouldn't be so much likelihood of my breaking anything.

I made it all the way down without falling. That didn't come until I was on the flat. I had hit the beach and I was headed for the abandoned flashlight. I was going to pick it up and have myself a look around. More than that, I was thinking that now there was nothing to keep me down on the beach. Quiet had broken out. The idiot loudmouths had scooted off across the bay and it seemed most unlikely that they would be coming back.

Since the flashlight had evidently been abandoned and it was just lying there on the beach running its battery dead, there was no reason why I shouldn't salvage it. It would be handy for getting myself back along the path up the bluff. When I had started down the path, I'd been expecting that for coming back up I would be going the long way around.

If you go along the beach to the mouth of the bay, you come to a place where the rocky bluff dwindles down and there's a road that circles in to skirt the beach. That's the long way around. The road would take me back to the house. With the light I'd have no need of going that way. I could go straight up by the path.

Only a step or two short of where I was going to reach down and pick the thing up, I came up against something that shouldn't have been there. It was big, and, when my foot struck against it, it yielded. It wasn't a rock. Rocks aren't soft unless they are Claes Oldenburg rocks. The thought passed through my mind, but it went out faster than it had come in. I was thinking that the thing was more like something baled up.

Anyhow it wasn't thinking time. I had barged into it and it was tripping me up. My feet went out from under me and I went sprawling on top of the thing. I landed in a face-down spraddle, but with that soft thing to cushion me I suffered no damage. My right hand was only inches away from the flashlight. Stretching a bit, I reached for it. My hand was expecting the feel of the smooth metal cylinder. Closing on the unexpected, my hand jumped away. I didn't bring it back in. I knew what it had touched and I knew what lay under me where I was sprawled. The flashlight wasn't lying abandoned on the beach. A man had it gripped in his hand. My fingers had closed over that hand. I was lying on a man's body.

I pulled myself up off it and, even as I was coming away, I was recognizing something more. I had come down hard on top of him and he hadn't moved or made a sound. I had lain sprawled all over him and I'd felt not even the slightest movement, not even the small rise and fall of breathing. Now I was having some misgivings about commandeering the flashlight.

I was facing up to a tricky decision. I was remembering the one shot. Every instinct I had was up and yelling at me that the man was dead. If dead, then it must follow that he was shot to death and the body would then be for the police. In such situations the police have a prejudice in favor of having their dead bodies left untouched. Rob-

bing the dead is a crime. Borrowing from the dead is
frowned upon. You don't mess around. You just call the
cops.

That was okay as far as it went, but my mind was
jumping way past it. Suppose he wasn't dead but just
wounded, or maybe even just sick. I'd heard the one shot,
but that didn't say he had been hit. He could have
fainted. He could have had a coronary. Shock and fright
can bring one on. My foot had hit against him, and I had
fallen all over him. There were some things I knew about
him. He was big and he had a lot of fat on him. I could
well imagine that he was just the type that goes walking
around looking for a coronary.

Wounded or sick would turn the whole thing around.
That way there would be every reason for touching him.
There would be every reason for grabbing the flashlight
away from him if only to look him over so I could know
whether there might still be a chance that anything could
be done for him.

I guess this sounds as though I just stood there in the
dark taking the better part of forever for thinking the
thing through and weighing the pros and cons while
maybe there on that dark beach the guy was breathing
his last. I may not be the world's quickest thinker, but in
times of stress thinking speeds up. It takes longer to tell
the thoughts than to think them. They jump at you and
on the jump you catch them.

The only reason I was standing there and giving it any
thought before I moved was because I was trying to
argue myself away from certainty. I was sure the guy was
dead. You can feel a body to find out whether it still has
any life in it. I'd had a lot more than a feel of this body. I
came to a decision. I needed that light more than he did.
If I was wrong about him and he was still alive, I needed

it for him. If I was right and the man was dead, even murdered, nobody could rate my taking the flashlight out of his hand as destruction of evidence. If the cops would want to be technical about it, they could call me stupid. That I could take.

I bent down and took the light out of his hand. He wasn't holding it in any rigid death grip. It just lay in his hand and his hand was limp. I didn't have to force his fingers open or anything like that. The light had shown me more of the dried-up seaweed than I could ever want to see. I turned the beam on the body.

He was dead. The hole in his shirt spoke for the way he'd died. It was the shot I'd heard. There had been only the one because only one had been needed. He was in uniform and he was wearing a shield. He was a cop. I have never seen a fatter one. You see that up in the north country. The natives seem to come in two breeds. They are either long muscled, lean, and wiry, or they run to lard. The fat ones seem to be nowhere fatter. I suppose it comes from hibernation through the long, hard winters.

For a moment or two, I stood there looking at him and kicking around the thought of putting the flashlight back into his limp hand and going down the beach to the road and back that way to the house and the telephone.

The next move would be to call the police and I was wondering whether there would be any police to call. It was a small town and at least since 1812 it had been a peaceful one. This one cop could have been all the force they had.

I came to a decision. I had taken the thing. If that was tampering, then to put it back and say I hadn't touched it would be worse than tampering. There was every reason for going up to the house the short way. I should have been getting to the phone and quick.

I started for the path up over the rocks and then I remembered Mathilda. I swept the beach with the light beam, looking for her while I was whistling her to me. Just then another light popped up and fell full on me.

CHAPTER 2

The timing couldn't have been neater. The guy who held that other light threw his beam on me just a fraction of a second before the swing of my light beam would have landed on him. He was standing there with Mathilda jumping around him. One hand was occupied with his flashlight. With the other he was fending off the pup's unsuitably affectionate advances. It was Creighton Douglas. In the few minutes of their meeting, when he had come to pick Millie up for dinner, Mathilda had gone for him in a big way. She'll do that. I've often thought that her judgment about people falls something short of being infallible.

"Hi," Douglas said. "What's been going on here?"

"Where's Millie?"

Capping a guy's question with one of your own is often just a way of dodging an answer, but that wasn't what I was doing. I thought that my question took precedence over his. I could see nothing more than curiosity behind what he was asking. My question was to the point, and he seemed to see it my way. He answered me and he didn't press me for any answer.

"In bed by now," he said. "She said she was going to fall right in. No hair brushing, no face creaming—she said she wasn't even going to stop long enough to wash her teeth."

I moved my light back onto the body. Douglas whistled. He came walking over and joined the beam of his light to mine.

"I heard a shot," he said. "Jesus! Poor Beebee."

"Town cop?"

"Yes. Burton Bean. Everybody calls him Beebee. You know where there's a stop sign up by the golf links, the place where there's the garage across the road?"

I knew the stop sign. It seemed wildly irrevelant.

"What about it?" I asked.

"Beebee was always up there. He'd sit in his car hiding behind the garage and drinking Coke after Coke just waiting for someone to go through without stopping so he could pop out and tag him. You'd think they were running the town on the fines. What could have brought him down here?"

"For that matter," I said, "what brought you down here?"

"Since you ask," he said, "I'd guess the same as you. It was the noise. There were some idiots down here carrying on fit to raise the dead. We heard them as we were coming up the road to the house. Millie was having a fit. She was sure they'd wake the general. So I promised her I'd do something about them as soon as I'd dropped her off. I drove back as far as the beach and walked in from the road. I heard the shot as I was coming in. It struck me that, if this was the way it was, I could be smarter if I didn't advertise myself with a light."

Just about the time he was telling me that, there was a new sound. It came from out on the bay. It was a series of loud splashes. They seemed loud enough to have been close, but I had a hunch that they weren't. When everything is still, sound will carry a long way over water.

I held my hand up, trying to turn him off so I could lis-

ten. He ignored me and just went on talking. By the time
he had finished, the sounds of splashing had stopped.

"Did you hear that out there?"

"A bunch of crazies skinny-dipping," he said. "They've
got to be crazy to have a boat sitting out there on the bay
without any riding lights."

"They took off from here without riding lights," I said,
"and that may be the one thing about them you couldn't
call crazy."

Douglas whistled again.

"You mean the ones who did Beebee?"

"We better hit a phone," I said. "If we can get through
to the police while those guys are still out there . . ."

"You go," Douglas said. "I'll stay here with poor old
Beebee and wait for them to come."

It never occurred to me to put up an argument about
which of us would go. I was, after all, the one who was
staying in the house and the nearest telephone was up
there. Also, now that he had come up close and we were
both standing over the body, Mathilda was also there and
she had taken to sniffing at the dead man. I was holding
her off and working at bringing her to heel, but it was
something of a struggle. It seemed a good idea to get her
away from there.

Doing it with a light made climbing the rock path up
to the lawn quick and easy. Back up on the flat I ran for
the house. Maybe I should have given nothing precedence over calling the cops but, without even thinking
about it, my first concern just then was for Sam. I took
the few moments it needed for looking in on him. He was
awake.

"Old bastards like me," he said, "we don't sleep well,
but what's your problem, Matt?"

"You sleep all right, you old bastard," I said. "All hell broke loose down on the beach and it woke me. You slept right through it."

"We old bastards don't hear well either," he said. "Noise doesn't wake me. Nothing does. I just wake myself. My kidneys take care of that for me."

"You all right?" I asked.

"Sure. What was it down on the beach?"

"I don't know. Laughing, hooting, yelling—it sounded like kid foolishness. You know, they've had more booze than they can handle or, even up here I suppose, marijuana or cocaine."

"Even up here," Sam said. "They just simmered down or you been doing something?"

"Neither. I went down there with the idea I would, but now I have to call the police. I should be on the phone right now. I'll tell you all about it after I've made the call."

"Is it all quiet," Sam said, "or is my hearing so much worse that I just think it's all quiet?"

"It's all quiet."

"Then let it lay, Matt. Beebee can hear about it in the morning. He's the lardass who's the law around here."

"He heard about it tonight, Sam. He's down there on the beach and he's dead. One shot right on target."

"Oh," Sam said. "More than kid nonsense then."

"A lot more but not without the nonsense element. They took off from the beach and they're out on the bay now. It sounds like they're skinny-dipping."

"Straight from killing a police officer? You better hit the phone."

I left him and I went to the telephone. I dialed the operator and asked her to put me through to the police. She moved fast. I heard the ringing almost immediately, but then I went on hearing it. It rang and rang and nobody was picking it up. It was a long time before she gave up on it and came back to me.

"He's out," she said. "Do you want me to keep ringing him? I'll get him when he comes back in and I'll ring you. He went out on a call and I guess he isn't back yet. He ought to be back soon, so if you want him tonight, I can call you or would you rather wait till morning now?"

"You talking about Bean?" I asked.

"Yes, Beebee. He's the town policeman. There isn't anyone else."

"Then it's no good waiting," I began.

The operator broke in on me.

"There's no way to reach him till he comes back in," she said.

"That's why it's no good waiting," I said. "Ring the State Troopers for me. Would you, please?"

She made a funny little sound. I read it for distress.

"Beebee isn't going to like it," she said. "It makes him mad if the troopers come horning in."

"I'll worry about that. You just get me the troopers."

"Are you calling for General Dalton?" she asked.

"He told me to make the call," I said.

It was true enough and it served the purpose. I gathered that I needed it to persuade her to do what I wanted since doing it was so clearly against her better judgment.

I heard the ringing start up again, and again it went on and on without any answer. It broke off and I was expecting that she would come back on to tell me that the state like the town had only one cop and that he was out somewhere. She didn't. The ringing resumed and now there was just a shade of difference in the tone of it and I got through even before it had started on the second ring.

She had been making a second try at Bean before she gave up and did as I had asked.

I hadn't been too comfortable in my mind about the few minutes I'd taken with Sam before going to the phone. I was thinking that those crazy goons wouldn't be sitting out there on the bay forever. My delay in getting in my report of the killing could have been giving them the time they would have needed for being off and away. I stopped thinking about those few minutes that I could lay at my own door. They were as nothing compared to the time the telephone operator had taken before she put me through to the State Troopers.

Once I was talking to them, the whole process speeded up. I gave them a quick account of what had been happening. As much as I was a quick talker, they were quick listeners. They took in everything the first time around. I didn't have to repeat anything for them or to explain anything. They knew the beach and they knew Sam's house and they knew Beebee Bean.

I held on while my report was being relayed to the officers who would be going out on the call. I could hear the man as he was filling them in and he was giving them the whole of it, getting every detail right. Having done that much, he came right back to me. The troopers would be right over. They would appreciate it if I remained by the phone till they arrived. It was just possible that they would want to speak to me.

I wasn't to expect them immediately. The State Police barracks were thirty-five miles away. Although they would be making good time, on the twisting country roads in the dark of the night thirty-five miles was a sizable piece of driving.

"We're relaying this through to the Coast Guard," the

man said. "If you get a call, it'll be more likely from them than from us. So please stick with the phone."

I said I would and I hung up. I headed back to Sam's room. I was going to tell him that I had gotten through to the troopers and that they had the thing in hand. When I got in there, however, he was sleeping again and I wasn't going to wake him just for that. I backed out and, when I turned from shutting the door behind me, I all but fell over Millie. She was out there, right by the door.

For a babe who was so beat that she was going to fall into bed without even stopping to brush her teeth, she looked more than alert. If she had ever made a start on that fall, she had done a complete reversal of direction. She was fully dressed, still wearing every last thing she'd had on when Creighton Douglas had picked her up for dinner early in the evening. She was wide-eyed, but she was also shaking.

"I heard you on the phone," she said. "I was listening on the kitchen extension."

"Why?"

"Curiosity. I thought it was just going to be a funny story—those crazy boys down on the beach."

"You know those crazy boys?" I asked.

"I thought I did. I thought it would have to be the motorcycle bunch. They live down Water Street way and along the road out past the Grange. If it's noisy enough and silly enough, it's always them. Everybody knows that, but now I'm not at all sure. It's horrible, Matt. Beebee was the most worthless sort of oaf, but that makes no difference. He was alive and now . . ."

Her voice trailed away into a whimper. I picked up on what she had been saying.

"Now you don't know," I said. I had her by the arm

and I took her away from Sam's door. She was hanging at the edge of hysteria. If she was going to start screaming, it would be better if he didn't hear her. "What's been changing your mind?" I asked.

"Beebee," she said. "They're bratty and they're stupid, but they don't shoot people. They're noisy and inconsiderate. When they're riding their motorcycles, they're a menace on the streets here in town and a menace out on the roads, but that's not shooting people."

"You could be wrong about them," I said.

"No. There's something else. Crate and I heard them when we were coming in and there was something I couldn't understand about it then."

"Like what?"

"There's the place where the road touches the beach. That would be where they would have left their motorcycles when they went down on the beach. We went by there and there was nothing, no motorcycles."

"They took off from the beach on a boat. So they didn't come on their motorcycles. They came on a boat."

"Yes. I heard you on the phone. You said a boat. It's that, too. Where would they get a boat? They're just about the only people around here who don't go out on the water. They're tied to their crazy motorcycles. You know what the people are like up this way, Matt. They live for their boats, and these idiots don't. It's that more than anything else that makes them alien. You wouldn't believe it. They were all of them born here right in town and they are outsiders."

"When Douglas dropped you off here at the house and went around to the beach to get them to pipe down, who was he expecting to find down there?"

"Them. If it's silly and it's noisy, everybody always thinks them."

"Even though you'd driven past the place where they would have left their motorcycles and there'd been no motorcycles?"

"I didn't think about that until later. After Douglas left me, then it came to me. I began to wonder about that—no motorcycles."

"So you were worried for Douglas and you didn't go to bed?"

"I wasn't tired and I thought about there being no motorcycles and that made me curious."

"He said you were beat and you were going to fall straight into bed."

She laughed. It was a small laugh and, if I've ever heard a forced one, that was it.

"Oh, I told him that. I wasn't going to let him come in, not this time of night."

I took note of the assumption that the guy might have expected to come in at this time of night. The rest followed. She hadn't gone to bed and then, when she'd heard the shot, she had started worrying. She wasn't ready to say that she'd been worrying about Douglas. I had been out and Mathilda as well. She had just been worried—worried about everyone and no one.

"Were you waiting for Douglas to come back and tell you about it?" I asked.

It was no business of mine even though I'd known her all the way up since diaper days, but what she'd said about putting on an act so she could get out of asking him to come in was sticking in my mind.

"He wouldn't. He knew I was mad at him."

That was interesting. I would have liked to have known the whys of it, but it was a question I didn't think I could ask and I was making no comment. There's only just so much privacy that an honorary uncle can allow himself to invade. Even though I was keeping my mouth shut, she was, however, reading my face.

"It's not what you're thinking," she said.

"I'm not thinking anything," I said.

It was almost true. I was trying not to.

"Of course you are. What it was is only this. I didn't want him going down there on the beach and making a fuss. They would know that he was fussing at them because of Sam and that was going to rebound onto us. It's the way they are. They'll make themselves a nuisance and they'll aim it at us."

I could make nothing of that. It might have been that I didn't know everything there was to know about this girl, but this much I did know. What she was saying was completely unlike her. It had to be. No kid who had Sam Dalton's blood in her veins would take the appeasement road and let a lot of stupid punks terrorize her.

"Better to let them wake Sam?" I asked. "Wasn't that making themselves enough of a nuisance?"

"They didn't wake him, did they?"

"They didn't, but I never thought he could sleep through it."

"You don't know. Sam's almost totally deaf in his left ear. He sleeps on his right side, and with his good ear buried in the pillow he hears nothing. There wasn't a chance that they would wake Sam. I told Crate as much but he was being stubborn about it. Nothing would do but that he go down there and straighten those bums out. There was no point to it. He was just strutting his manhood for me and I can take only so much of that macho crap."

"I went down there, too," I said. "I was going to straighten them out."

"That's different. You didn't know about Sam's ear and there was nobody to tell you."

I suggested that she go to bed. I was going to wait up for the troopers and for a Coast Guard call if there was going to be one. It didn't need the both of us.

"I'll wait with you," she said.

"Look. I've had some sleep. You haven't had even a wink. Come tomorrow, you'll be dragging."

"I have nothing on for the morning. I can sleep late."

It was August, but it was also Penobscot Bay. You can get good hot days in that Down East country in August, but you always have cool nights and in the hours before dawn it will be more than cool. About that time of night you'll be pulling up the third blanket. She shivered.

"You are beat," I said. "It makes you feel the cold."

"I feel the cold because it is cold. I'll get a sweater."

She was gone only a few moments and she came back with one of those big, thick Norwegian ski jobs pulled on over her dress. It covered her almost to the knees, but the rest of the way down to her shoes it was the cascade of filmy skirt. It was so new a look that fashion may never catch up with it.

She went to the hall closet and came back with a padded scarlet jacket. I knew the thing. It was Sam's. He used to wear it in the woods in the fall, when he would go out after pheasant or deer. I wished she hadn't brought it out. I didn't like thinking that Sam would never be wearing it again.

"Do something for me, Matt," she said.

I thought she'd brought the jacket out for me to put on. I didn't need it and I didn't want it. I'd gone down to the beach with nothing on me from the waist up, but some time after I'd returned to the house—I couldn't remember when—I had hauled on a cashmere pullover. One of those keeps you plenty warm, particularly when you wear it right against your skin.

"I've got this thing on," I said. "I'm plenty warm enough."

"I know," she said. "It's Crate. He's wearing a light jacket. He'll be freezing down there on the beach. I thought if you wouldn't mind, you could take this down to him and make him put it on. Then send him up here before he catches his death. I'll make some hot cocoa to warm him up. There's nothing like it. If you think someone has to be down there with Beebee, couldn't you for just a little while? The troopers can't be much longer."

"Keep Mathilda here. Why don't I take some whiskey down to him? That and the jacket will take care of him."

She shook her head.

"No whiskey," she said. "He was drinking all evening. He's had enough. But you don't have to bother. I'll change my shoes and I'll go down."

"Hold it. Hold it," I said. "I'm going."

"And you will make him come up for the cocoa? He'll need it. I know."

"If you must play mamma," I said, "all right. I'll spell him down there. If the Coast Guard or the troopers call, have them hang on and go down to the lawn and yell for me if they aren't happy about giving you a message."

"Leave it to me," she said. "I'll hold the fort."

I took the padded jacket and picked up a flashlight. On a second thought I also took the one I had lifted out of Beebee Bean's hand. I wasn't going to pretend I hadn't touched it, but I could set things up to be much as they had been before I touched.

As I was going down through the garden and across the lawn, I was trying to talk myself out of feeling the way I did. If she was so dead set on getting Creighton Douglas up to the house and having some time alone with him that she was ready, as an alternative, to go down to the beach to be alone with him there, there wasn't much reason for my feeling like a pimp when I was only keeping her from going out in the cold.

When I had reached the end of the lawn, I called down to Douglas and I had no answer. Standing at the edge of the bluff, I played my light down on the beach. It seemed strange that I should need it. It seemed hard to believe that Douglas wouldn't have had his own light on, that he would be down there standing watch in the dark. Even as I was wondering about it, my mind popped up with what seemed the obvious answer. No light and no answer to my shout. Flashlight batteries are not inexhaustible. It wasn't impossible that his had run out during the wait down there on the beach. With regard to his failing to answer when I hailed him, Millie'd said that he had been drinking all evening. She'd even said that he'd had too much. So now he would be out flat somewhere down there, sleeping it off.

My light played over Beebee's body and the rags of seaweed. Everything seemed quite as I had left it except that in no sweep of my light beam could I pick up a sleeping sentry. I took the path down the bluff and I tried it on the beach. Douglas was nowhere in sight. I moved off fifty yards in both directions, up the beach and down, and either way at any point where he might have been and have still kept the corpse in sight there was no trace of him.

I couldn't help thinking of Millie making hot cocoa up at the house and waiting for the oaf to come up there to her, but I just couldn't see myself walking away from the body and leaving it lying there with nobody watching it.

I recognized that it had already been that way for some indeterminate time, but then I hadn't known it. I had at first sight formed a low opinion of Creighton Douglas and now with every moment it was dropping steadily lower.

I climbed back up to the top of the bluff and shouted for Millie. Since she had briefed me on Sam's deafness, I was no longer worried about any need to hold it down to where it would run no risk of waking him. Faced east toward the house I saw a light rim along the horizon where dawn had begun the bleaching of the sky. Suddenly it wasn't as dark as it had been. Light, although it was still coming thinly, was coming fast.

Millie came out of the house and came down through the garden toward me. There wasn't enough light yet to make her out as she moved among the roses and the snowballs and the stocks, but she was coming with a flash and I could see that. She came out to the lawn.

"What's the matter?" she said. "Won't he come?"

"He's not down there. It looks like he just took off."

She said nothing till she had crossed the lawn and was standing beside me. Perched at the edge of the bluff, she took her turn at playing her light over the beach. When the beam picked up the dead cop's body, she held it in a moment of pause, but it was only a moment; and when she came away from it, it was convulsively. She was snatching the light away from the body. Though for a few moments more she kept scanning the beach, she was now manipulating her light with care. She didn't want to bring Beebee's corpse into sight again.

"He's gone home and gone to bed," she said. "I suppose it's a good thing that at least one of us should be sensible."

"Sensible is one thing you might call it," I said. "That's your word. I have another."

"Like what?"

"Like rotten."

She laughed.

"That too, but it's old stuff. Sensible is new."

I wanted to ask why she gave the guy any time if that was what she thought of him; but I had already asked so many questions, and I was looking ahead to so many more, that it seemed to me it could quickly come to be too much and I would do better to hold it down to the clearly relevant. So some of it was self-control, but I cannot pretend that self-control didn't get an assist from interruption.

Several lights, and powerful ones, popped up on the beach. The State Troopers had arrived. We went down the rocky path to meet them. Things at the very first were a little confused because they thought I was Douglas. It was natural. The way they had it programmed, I would be up in the house holding down the phone and Douglas would be on the beach waiting with the body. They had no way of knowing that there was nobody up above at the phone.

We got that straightened around. I was Erridge. I was the guy who had called them. I wasn't Creighton Douglas.

"Then where is Mr. Douglas?"

Millie answered that one.

"I suppose he got tired and cold down here," she said. "He went home to bed."

"Where does Mr. Douglas live?"

She told them. From what she said I couldn't pinpoint the house, but I knew the town and its surrounding area well enough to form a good general idea of where it was. The troopers were right in there along with me.

"From here, a mile and a half," one said.

"Or more," said his partner.

"About that," Millie said. "Only a few minutes' drive."

She might have added that the way he drove it would have been even shorter than any State Trooper could think, but she left that unsaid. I said nothing.

"But a long walk and a long hill to climb," the first trooper said. "For a man who's so dog-tired that he runs out on what he's undertaken to do, it's a very long walk."

"Creighton Douglas," Millie said. "He never in his whole life walked anywhere. If he has to go fifty feet, he'll jump in his car."

"What does he drive?"

"It's a Jaguar."

"Vanity license: 'CRATE'?"

"That's it."

"His car, miss, is down there. It's parked where the road comes down to the beach."

CHAPTER 3

The troopers took over on the body. They worked me for a statement and they worked Millie for a statement. Since they were interested in her witnessing, even though it gave them nothing more than her having heard the sounds of revelry and then the shot that knocked them off, I decided that I was obliged to volunteer the one small additional contribution I was able to make.

"If you want to talk to everyone who heard it," I said, "there's somebody else. Someone else heard it."

They thought I was talking about Creighton Douglas. They reminded me that they were going to have to find him before they could question him.

"Not Douglas," I said. "Someone else. The telephone operator will probably know who."

I had to explain that. It was, of course, only something I had pieced together, but there didn't seem to be any reason for doubting my patchwork. When I had been trying to reach the local police, not knowing that Beebee Bean had been all of it, the operator had told me that there had been a call and that Bean had gone out on it and that, therefore, we could expect no answer on his telephone until he returned.

It certainly followed that, since this call had taken him down to the beach, the call must have been a complaint about the noise and activity on the beach. The troopers were less certain of it. They suggested another possibility.

The call that had taken the town cop out could have been anything. If, going to take care of it, he had in passing heard the uproar, he might very well on his own have gone in to investigate.

"His car is parked back there on the road, right in front of Douglas'."

It had, of course, been obvious all along that it would be there. Just from the mass and volume of his remains, anyone would have known that Officer Beebee Bean had been a man who never walked anywhere when he could ride. Even if it hadn't been a town-owned car and tax-payer-provided gas, Beebee would never have walked.

Once they had brought up their possible alternative, however, and had deflated Erridge, they did something of a turnaround. Obviously, if I was right in the assumption I'd been making, the town police car would now be parked where they had found it. Bean would have driven there and then walked in to investigate.

Thanking us for our cooperation, they said there was no need for keeping us from our beds any longer. I had no urge to return to mine. The sun was up and, although I hadn't had a full night's sleep, I was not feeling the need of any more. Millie, so far as I knew, hadn't been to bed at all and, if she had, it would not have been for sleeping. I wasn't disposed to check into that. She was a big girl. She had to be left to manage her own life.

I expected, however, that belatedly now she would be doing that falling into bed Douglas had said she so sorely wanted. She was shivering. Her teeth were chattering. Back in the house, though, she headed for the kitchen. We were to have that cocoa and there would be brandy in it. She insisted that we needed it. Since her need was obvious, I went along with her on it.

I was watching while she started making it.

"Matt," she said, "do something for me."

Her tone was telling me that this would be an important something.

"Like what?" I asked.

"Call Crate," she said. "Just to make sure he's all right."

"Why don't you call him yourself?"

"If he isn't home—and I can't see him leaving his car and walking all that way—it will be embarrassing if I call."

"You don't think he'll be home?"

"It's not like him and since Beebee was killed down there . . ."

"Any reason why he should have been killed too?"

"It's crazy, I know, but he was down there alone and it's crazy Beebee being killed. Stupid kids are having a noisy beach party. He goes to the beach to tell them to tone it down. He gets killed for that?"

"There's only the one body down there," I said.

"I know, but it's frightening. Please call him for me. If you get him, I'll talk."

There was a phone book on the shelf below the kitchen extension. I reached for it, but Millie had the phone number ready in her head. She gave it to me, and I dialed it.

So there I was again, hanging on to the phone and listening to the repeated ringing. It took a long succession of rings before the phone was picked up and then it was a woman's voice. She came on swinging. There was no "hello," no "Douglas residence," none of the conventional phone-answering gambits.

Her words need no repetition. She had the vocabulary of an enraged truck driver, limited but vivid, and she reached down into it to fling at the phone its most obscene and blasphemous items. It was the middle of the night and only the misbegotten would murder sleep at that hour. Waiting till she had run out of breath, I hurried into the first moment of lull to ask if I might speak to Creighton Douglas.

She should have known that the call would be for him. The people she knew were sane. Nobody she knew would ever commit the outrage of calling anybody at that hour.

"Hold on," she said. "I'll go wake him. This is just like that precious husband of mine. He's pulled a pillow over his ear and gone on sleeping. I know him."

I held on. She was gone only briefly.

"He's not here," she said. "His bed hasn't been slept in, so he's jumped into another bed tonight, and I think I know which one."

She gave me a number, and with an ear-shattering bang she hung up. It was a number I couldn't help knowing. It was, after all, the only local number I had over the years called with any frequency. Even if I hadn't known it, I had it right there in front of me on the phone I was using. I hung up.

"Not there?" Millie asked. "Did she say whether he'd been in and gone out again?"

"She said his bed hadn't been slept in. She gave me a number where I could reach him."

Handling it as though I didn't know, I repeated the number for her.

"Dear, sweet, foul-mouthed Marian," she said.

There was an awkward silence. I should say perhaps that it was awkward for me. Millie gave no sign of being discomfited. I moved away from it. I had a good reason to offer for a short absence. I was going to look in on Sam, just in case Dexter had still not come in.

Sam was alone and he was awake. He said he was all right and there was nothing he wanted. I stayed with him. He commented on my being early up and I filled

him in on the events of the night. Sam found none of it
baffling. He had ready explanations for the whole deal.
Millie joined us, bringing the chocolate and brandy. She
wanted to get Sam something, but there was nothing he
wanted or needed. We sat by his bedside and sipped the
drink she had made. It was as warming as she had promised it would be. Meanwhile, Sam was giving us his estimate of the situation.

According to his way of thinking, Millie was wrong
about the motorcycle gang. They were witless enough to
have done all that hooting and hollering in the middle of
the night, and they were savage enough and enough
undisciplined to have shot that gross idiot of a policeman
for nothing more than having had the effrontery to tell
them to pipe down.

"You know what they are, Matt," he said. "They're the
generation you can say are the younger brothers of the
veterans back from Vietnam. You and I, we know what a
war does to kids. You just can't run a war without cor-
rupting the boys you've got fighting it. Even in a good
war, what do they learn? They learn to dodge respon-
sibility. They learn to pass the buck. They learn to do the
very least they can get away with. On top of all that, they
learn to kill. That's even in a good war. In Vietnam they
learned to kill their officers. They come back, and in the
eyes of these kids ten years younger, they're great stuff.
So a big blob of lard wearing a uniform hits the beach
and starts giving these kids orders. In Vietnam their
elders did it to men who were a lot better than Beebee
Bean. For this lot, Beebee was just about the right size.
Silly, undisciplined, and vicious, and let's not pretend
that they aren't what we deserve."

I'd heard this kind of thing from Sam before. He had
never been happy about the draft. His acceptance of it as

a wartime necessity had never been better than grudging. It was his idea that, although you could make usable troops out of draftees, they could never be what he was willing to call soldiers. Sam had always argued that, since they were not true soldier material, the military experience didn't shape them. Inevitably it corrupted them.

He was equally ready with his explanation of the strange behavior of Creighton Douglas.

"Would you expect anything else of him?" he asked.

"But, Sam," Millie said, "Matt left him down there to watch over the body till the troopers would come. Then, when they came, he wasn't there and he hadn't used his car to go anywhere else and he hasn't gone home. So, if you know what was to have been expected of him, you tell me where he is."

"It was to have been expected that he wouldn't have the stomach to stay where he should have been. It was cold out there. It wasn't comfortable and Creighton Douglas has to have his comfort. It also got spooky alone there in the dark with the dead body. The man is soft and the man is yellow. Nobody should have expected that he would stay the course. He's just behaving in character."

I was thinking that Millie might have shown some resentment of that. She had, after all, been dating the guy. Wouldn't you have thought she might rise to his defense? She didn't rise at all. She was taking every one of Sam's accusations as self-evident.

"I know what you mean," she said, "but then where is he?"

"Someplace safe and someplace warm and comfortable," Sam said. "You can bet on that. He'll come out of it in good time with a story of how all this time he was snooping around or something, heroically trying to run Bean's killer to ground."

Her lips twitched. She almost giggled. So far as I could see, her own opinion of Creighton Douglas was no more favorable than was Sam's. How I was to match that up with the fact that she dated the guy and that now she was full of concern for his safety, I just didn't know.

"I think the time has come," she said, "when I shall stop seeing Mr. Creighton Douglas. He was all right for passing the time, but perhaps I can do better with a good book."

"Even with a bad book," Sam said.

"Sam, darling," Millie said, "you're a horrid old man."

"Of course, I am. What else is there left for me to be? You wouldn't want me to be a senior citizen."

"Lord forbid."

For some time she had been fighting down yawns, and increasingly it was a losing fight. Along about then, Dexter turned up and said something about getting Sam ready for the day. Dexter wasn't looking his prettiest. His eyes were red-rimmed and bloodshot, and there was a gray tinge to his face. He had a bad case of the morning-after look, but he was freshly shaved and, as he came into the room, he was running the comb through his hair.

Millie picked up her cup and mine.

"My signal to leave," she said. "I'm going to lie down for a while."

"Make it the whole morning," Sam said. "You go on missing sleep, you'll get to look like Dexter. One of him is enough."

Dexter forced one of his isn't-the-old-man-cute laughs. Standing at the bedside and reaching for the bedcovers as though ready to start on the things he had to do for

Sam, he looked at me. It was a pointed look. It was telling me that, if I also would take myself out of there, he could get on with it. I headed for the door.

"You don't have to go, Matt," Sam said.

Dexter took his hand away from the bedclothes. He was scowling.

"Not if you want me to stay," I said.

Turning his back on Sam, Dexter took a shot at explaining him to me.

"I'll call you when we're finished," he said. "The general doesn't like having anybody around to watch."

Sam glared at the man's back.

"As you were," he said. "The general speaks for himself."

"But you know you . . ." Dexter began.

"You do your job," Sam said. "I'll do my own thinking."

"It's going to be one of those days when he's difficult," Dexter said.

"It's going to be one of those days when you'll do better to watch your step," I said.

Dexter muttered something. Since it escaped me, Sam certainly couldn't have heard it. I let it go. The guy never relaxed his scowl and he went on muttering to himself all the time he was getting Sam out of his pajamas and giving him a bed bath. He worked quickly and efficiently. It was obvious that he knew his job and did it well. It was painful watching. Sam, through all the years I had known him, had been a lot of man. Now there was little left and that little so helpless.

I watched Dexter do the back rub. The man was still in a foul temper. His rage showed in his face but, despite it, he was performing well. He wasn't taking any of his fury out on Sam. I wondered whether it might have been different if I hadn't been there watching. The disparity between the strength of the man's hands and arms and poor Sam's enfeebled and depleted body could have been frightening. Dexter could all too easily have taken Sam Dalton in his hands and broken him in two.

Sam all the while kept riding him.

"You stretched your evening into a night off," he said.

"I got back later than usual. You said you wouldn't be needing me with your friend here."

"You didn't get back at all, not till morning."

"Not in here, no. There was a note on the door, telling me to keep out. . . ."

"What note? What door?"

I had to step into that. Sam was on the way to calling the guy a liar. I couldn't let him go out on a limb he would only have to back off of.

"I came in here to sleep, Sam," I said. "I tacked a note to the door telling him I was in here and I would be with you through the night."

Sam heard me out, but he wasn't through with Dexter.

"And you took that as your signal to pull back out again and take off the rest of the night?"

"I could have. I wasn't needed, but as a matter of fact I didn't. I just slept in my own room. I was in the house if you'd needed me."

"How long in the house? You look as if you hadn't slept a week."

"So I'm hung over. Too much booze and six hours' sleep wasn't nearly enough recovery time, and six hours was all I had before it was time to get you started on your day. What did you want me to do? Stay in the sack and leave it for your friend to do all this for you?"

The guy was preening himself on his fidelity to duty. I looked at my watch. It was just coming up on eight o'clock. He had already been a good half hour ministering to Sam, and he had made his appearance freshly showered and shaved and with everything zipped and buttoned. Subtract six hours from seven-thirty and something before, and friend Dexter had my note turning him away from Sam's door at some time between one and one-thirty.

It had been after two when I'd written the note and tacked it to the door. The guy was stretching the truth a little but, despite the fact that he was an obnoxious twerp, it could hardly be easy to find another who would be as good as Dexter at his job. The idiot had exactly what Sam needed.

Listening to him, I kept setting up marks against him. Watching him, as he worked over Sam, I was setting up the coutervailing marks that many times overwhelmed all discernible negative aspects. This wouldn't be the first time that a man who had overstayed his leave tried to mitigate it by shaving the time by some minutes or even by an hour.

I could hardly figure him for being an inexperienced liar, but he was an inept one. Clara called from the far side of the bedroom door to ask me if she should bring me a breakfast tray when she brought the general his.

"Miss Millie isn't getting up for any breakfast," she said, "and Dexter already had his, so I been thinking if maybe you'd rather not be eating alone. It's no trouble for me either way."

Sam answered for me. I was silently adding to my calculations the time it would take to snatch even the quickest breakfast.

"Bring it in here, Clara," Sam said. "I want the company."

She brought our breakfasts and Sam shooed Dexter out of the room. Before the man left, he set out on Sam's bed tray a little row of pills and capsules. As soon as we were alone, Sam gathered them up into the palm of his hand and dropped them into the wastepaper basket that he had standing beside his bed.

"Come on, General," I said. "That isn't where they go."

"It's where I put them."

"Does your doctor know?"

"Not him and not Millie. They'd just fuss at me."

"So now I'm fussing at you, Sam."

"Since when are you an old lady, Matt?"

"Since when are you an old fool, Sam?"

"Can you ask? Since I got to the place where I can't do for myself and I have to keep that idiot around to wipe my ass for me."

"If you have a doctor and you don't think he knows what he's doing, you switch to another doctor. You don't keep him on and play this kind of game with him."

"He's a good doctor. He knows what he's doing."

"So how come you know better?"

"Because I don't pretend and he thinks he has to. I've lived too long, Matt. I asked him what all that crap is for. Is it to keep me alive? He's an honest man, so he wouldn't say it was for that. He said it will just keep me feeling better. So having your company makes me feel better and without any of that."

"If you're doing this because I'm here," I said, "maybe I should take the rest of my breakfast out to the dining room."

"When you aren't here, I think up other reasons. When a man has to depend on the chemists for feeling good, he's better off feeling bad."

"Who empties your wastepaper basket?"

"The idiot."

"Dexter?"

"I don't surround myself with any more idiots than I need. You see, Matt, there's nothing so bad that there isn't some good in it. This here now is the good of Dexter's idiocy. He never thinks to check on what I throw away."

"You shouldn't have told Clara to bring my breakfast in here."

"I'm long past thinking about should or shouldn't. I'm a self-indulgent old bastard."

"Indulging yourself in not feeling good?" I asked.

"It's a paradox, Matt. When you're living too long, all your living is a paradox. This one luxury I can grab off for myself, just this one little thing that lets me feel that even to this small extent I am still master of myself."

"It's a dirty trick on your doctor. You're putting him off in all his calculations of your condition. You've got him working on false assumptions."

"No, I'm not," Sam said. "It's the other way around. I'm keeping him from making me go along on false assumptions. Those things are just placebos. They're not for me. They're for fools and children."

"And if not?"

"If they are for me? If I'm wrong about myself and I am a child or an imbecile?"

"If they are something more than placebos, Sam. Wouldn't it be better if you just told the doctor you won't take them? Have it out with him. Why wouldn't that make you feel master of yourself? Mastery by stealth and deception, Sam? Since when has that been your style?"

"Since always, Matt. I was a strategist, kid, or wasn't I?"

"You were and the best there was."

"Don't exaggerate. I wasn't bad. I was good enough to

know the score. What is strategy if it isn't stealth and deception?"

"Worked on the enemy, Sam. Who's your enemy?"

"Millie."

"Millie?"

"Yes, because she loves me and I love her. That gives her leverage on me. When you're old and helpless, anyone who has leverage on you is the enemy."

"Then I'm also the enemy, Sam, because, you old bastard, I love you, too."

"You're not going to tell Millie?"

"No, but I'm going to talk to your doctor."

"No good ordering you not to?"

"No good, Sam. I'm a civilian now."

"And I'm out to pasture. What about if I ask you not to?"

"No good, Sam. I'll do this. I'll ask him not to tell Millie. I'll ask him to keep it private, just between you and him."

Sam sighed.

"If you must," he said.

"I must. If our places were switched, you would."

Sam grinned. It was a rueful grin, but there was some trace of fun in it.

"If our places were switched," he said, "I'd stuff them into your mouth and make you swallow."

"Not if our places were switched, Sam. You wouldn't then. You wouldn't any more than I will."

"Yes," he said. "Of course not." He changed the subject. "Talk about something good in everything," he said. "Even last night if it has put Millie off the Crate."

We talked some more, but mostly it was Sam talking and me just being an ear. His eyes were beginning to

close, and now and again he would drop off for a moment
or two. Those moments of sleep became more frequent
until the time came when he fell into a lasting nap. Those
naps came several times a day and, when he was properly
corked off, you'd tiptoe out of the room and leave him to
it.

This time I delayed my tiptoe for a quick look at the
pill bottles Dexter had sitting on top of a chest. The la-
bels gave me what I wanted. The doctor's name was
Buller. I didn't have to ask anybody or get into any
discussions. Finding Dr. Buller on my own was going to
be no problem. The phone book gave me his office ad-
dress. That was easy since his office was on the Common.
That put it not far from the hospital.

When I started out, Mathilda, of course, wanted to
come along. I told her I was headed for a doctor who
wasn't a vet and she was going to have to stay in the car
and behave herself while I would be busy with the doctor. She put on her most convincing good-dog expression
and I took her with me.

The doctor had a friendly receptionist. When I told her
I hadn't come as a patient but only to take a few minutes
of his time to talk with him about General Dalton, she
looked pained.

"But Dr. Buller won't talk about a patient," she said.
"Doctors don't, you know. It's a question of ethics."

"But I don't want him to talk," I said. "I talk. He
listens. Ethics don't say he can't listen."

She looked doubtful. It was obvious that this was a
young woman who hated to say no to anyone. I wondered if that abhorrence also applied in her private life.

"I'm sorry, Mr. Erridge," she said. "But you must understand that the doctor cannot accept any interference
in the doctor-patient relationship."

"Obviously not," I said. "It's not a matter of interference. It is only information. There is something about
Dr. Buller's patient that the doctor should know. Not
knowing, the doctor is working at a disadvantage."

"I don't know."

I had moved her from the flat no to a hesitation.

"Just tell me when the doctor will be in," I said. "He
can decide whether he will give me a few moments or
not."

On that basis she came through. The doctor had office
hours at eleven-thirty. I could come back then, but I was
not to think I had a guarantee that he would see me. She
was making no promises.

Mathilda had waited in the car. I gave her a run
around the Common. Then, leaving the Porsche parked
by Dr. Buller's office, I walked her down to the town
dock. She likes the dock. It's a place of rich and interesting smells. The lobstermen come in there with the day's
catch, and it is there that the fishing boats make their
landings. Visiting pleasure boats and a lot of those that
belong to residents of the town make their anchorages off
the dock. Only the bigger of the waterfront properties are
complete with boathouses and private docks.

Fully occupied with all that flavorful inhaling, Mathilda was giving me no mind. Out at the end of the dock
I spotted the State Trooper who had taken charge during
the night. He was in conversation with a young fellow
who was all beard and Coast Guard uniform. Looking my
way, the trooper waved a greeting. I didn't know
whether or not it was an invitation to join them, but I
took it as such.

I strolled over and Trooper Boudreau introduced me to
the Coast Guardsman. His name was Phil England. He
and the trooper were on Phil-and-Steve terms. England

had a good seagoing face to go with the seagoing whiskers. They were both noticeably blear-eyed, two men who were long overdue for their bunktime.

"How's it going?" I asked.

"It isn't," Boudreau said. "We're coming up empty all around."

"By the time we got out on the call, the boat was off and away," England said. "There was nothing moving anywhere on the bay and nothing up the river. The first movement was the lobstermen coming out to their traps in the morning."

He sounded apologetic. I couldn't see that he had any reason for it.

"There wasn't much chance that they'd be around long enough to let you catch up with them," I said. "There was only one thing that made it seem possible and even that wasn't much of a hope."

"What thing?" England asked.

"They were silly enough to be sitting out on the bay without running lights while they went swimming. If they had been idiotic enough or spaced out enough to have made it a long swimming party, you could have had them, but I had a hunch, even at the time, that it would be only a quick swim and then up and away. That's cold water and the air was getting colder by the minute. It had to be that the cold would bring them to their senses and they would begin to realize what they had done. They had just killed a cop. It had to come to them that it was the wrong place and the wrong time for horsing around."

"You're sure they went swimming?" England asked.

"You know how sound carries over the water. I heard a series of splashes. They came one after another in quick succession, guys jumping off a boat. I even have a count I think I can be sure of—four guys. There were four splashes. The thing is that was all I heard. So it wasn't the way that sort of thing would usually go. You know, guys dive in. They swim around a little and then they climb back out and take a moment's breather before they dive in again. I didn't hear any of that, no diving in again. But, as I was saying, it was the only chance and there was never much hope of it."

England turned to Boudreau.

"We went right out on your call and we hit the area in record time," he said.

"You did," I said. "I saw your lights. You were far quicker than I ever imagined you could be." I turned to Boudreau. "The trouble was all the delay before I called you. They had all the time they needed and more while I was fooling around with trying to rouse the town police. If I had known that the dead cop down on the beach was all the town police there was, there wouldn't have been that delay."

Boudreau sighed. "Yeah," he said. "And to make it worse, the whole thing makes no sense. We came down on the motorcycle bunch. There are five of them and they always do everything in a pack, all five. You counted four guys diving in."

England didn't think much of that bit.

"One of them maybe wasn't so crazy about cold water," he said. "It could have been the five and only four going in."

"Also," I said, "I can't guarantee my four count. I wasn't concentrating on the number. It could have been five."

"They alibi each other which, of course, isn't worth a

dime, but they say they weren't anywhere near the bay all night and they don't have any boats. They have motorcycles."

"They admit they were out? Not home tucked up in bed?"

"That's where they were when we went after them, but none of them even tried to pretend he had been in for long."

"Was that honesty?" I asked. "Or was it just that they couldn't be sure their families would back them up on a lie?"

"That and they could have been sure that there hadn't been nearly enough time for their motorcycles to have cooled down. Every last one of them was hot."

CHAPTER 4

"If they were roaring around town on their motorcycles at that time of night, wouldn't people have been wakened? No complaints?"

"Probably not," Boudreau said. "It's been going on too long. People have gotten tired of complaining. Also if there were any complaints, they would have gone to Bean; and he wasn't around to complain to. Even if he was, we can't look for him to be telling us about it now."

The story the troopers had from the motorcyclists offered only the most slender possibility of verification. They said they had been racing each other. It had been something like an impromptu rally, and they had staged it on stretches of road well away from any houses and separated by miles from the beach.

"We know these kids," Boudreau said. "There isn't a chance we wouldn't know them. It's a couple of years now they've been a nonstop pain in the ass. Any kind of hell-raising you want to name, they do it. There isn't a one of them hasn't been picked up at least a half a dozen times except that I can't remember when it hasn't been all five of them at once. We pick them up and we shake them down. There's never been a gun on any of them. Up in these parts when, come the fall, everybody's out after deer, and there's some that don't even wait for the season, they're different. They freak out on the motorcycles. It's hard to figure them for shooting anyone."

"Crazy kids," England said. "You never know. First it's just hell-raising and then it's worse."

"Maybe, but the guys we want weren't on motorcycles. They were in a boat. Where would they get a boat and where were the motorcycles?"

"They could steal a boat."

"Nobody's missing one. We've had no reports," Boudreau said.

"Fool around on it through the night and return it to its anchorage." England wouldn't be convinced.

"Like kids take a car just to go joy riding and then they return it or abandon it someplace where it can be found." Boudreau was thinking aloud. "No," he said. "It's not like them. It's out of their league. They don't carry guns. They're a nuisance. They annoy people. So anything, it goes around here, they're the ones get blamed."

"I'd haul the lot of them in anyway," England said.

Boudreau shook his head.

"They're not going anywhere. We can't pull guys in when we have nothing to hold them on, not just because they happen to be unpopular."

Up on the hill on Main Street the curbsides were filling up with parked cars. I looked at my watch. It was just past eleven, the time when people gathered at the post office to pick up the mail. Six mornings a week from eleven to eleven-thirty it was like a town meeting. The postmistress shut down her window while she sorted the mail into the boxes, and the townspeople gathered in the post office to wait and to catch up on the day's gossip.

I whistled Mathilda away from the interesting smells and we walked up the hill. As was to have been expected, there was only the one topic of conversation in the post office—the murder of Beebee Bean. Opinion seemed to be unanimous.

There was no understanding what the State Troopers could be thinking of. The town, stripped of any police protection of its own, lay open to every variety of unimaginable outrage. Everybody seemed to be forgetting that Beebee Bean, as protector of their security and safety, had never been anything more than an incongruously big-bellied slender reed.

He was gone and the town now had nobody. It was dependent on the State Troopers and who were they? They were outsiders. It wasn't their lives that were threatened. It wasn't their families in jeopardy. It wasn't their homes. They didn't care.

Those motorcycle ruffians had always been bad enough, but now the town was standing naked before their fury. What were the troopers waiting for? It wasn't as though there could be any doubt about who in their town belonged to the bad element. Why hadn't they all been rounded up and put away?

There was one word on every lip and that was "permissiveness." Gentle old ladies were urging that the men of the town take the law into their own hands. They didn't know why they were paying taxes. They were getting nothing for their tax money. I had a hunch that, if the town fathers erected a whipping post and a gallows on the Common, that would make them feel that they were getting something for their tax money.

I was saying nothing. I was just listening. Like the State Troopers, I was an outsider. Since I had been going to be up near the post office, I had taken the letterbox key with me when I'd left the house. I was waiting around to pick up the mail. When it would be time for me to return to the doctor's office, the mail sorting would have been finished.

A woman came swinging into the post office. It was evident that she was not an outsider. Just about everybody greeted her. Her response to the greetings couldn't have been more offhand. She stood just inside the door looking the people over. She seemed to be looking for one specific person. She was a husky woman, tall and angular and weather-beaten. She looked like something that had been left so long out in the sun that all the juice had dried out of her.

Her hair was silver blond, one of those hair colors that makes no pretense of being anything but a bottle job. Except for the brown of her skin and the pale tint of her hair, she was all pink—pink lacquered nails on fingers and toes, pink sandals, skin-tight pink pants, a pink shirt, and pink coral earrings.

The pants were low slung and the V of the shirt plunged all the way down to the low waistband. She was wearing no bra, but, beyond showing the world that the skin of her breasts was as brown and dry-looking as her face and her arms and her ankles, she was showing nothing. It was impossible to make any sure guess at her age. The best indication was the way she moved. I was inclined to put it somewhere in the forties. Through a mistaken effort to look sixteen, she looked more like sixty, but muscular and in good shape. In every detail she was gotten up for sex, and no woman could have looked less sexy.

Having surveyed the assembled company, she fixed her scrutiny on me. I knew at once that I had been chosen. There was no mistaking it. She worked her way through the crowded post office until she was standing face to face with me. When she spoke, I wondered why she had bothered to come so close. Her voice was a hoarse contralto with the carrying power of an old-fashioned orator's trumpeting. She addressed herself to me, but she was making certain that there wouldn't be an ear in the whole post office that wouldn't be taking in what she had to say.

"You're the man who's up here for the deathwatch on old Sam Dalton," she said.

"I'm visiting the general," I said, bringing my voice up to match the decibel level of hers. If we were to put on a show, I wasn't going to be the method actor mumbling unintelligibly.

"What's left of him," she said. "I'm Marian Douglas—Mrs. Creighton Douglas."

"Now am I supposed to say: 'Glad to meet you, Marian Douglas,' since I'm not?"

"I'm going to ask you to do something for me."

"Any reason why I should?"

"Any reason why you shouldn't?"

"Cruelty—yours. Bad manners—yours."

"Fiddlesticks. All I'm asking is that you take a message to Creighton. He is to let me know today whether he wants me to send his clothes over to the general's house. Unless I've heard from him before tomorrow, I shall have the Salvation Army people come and take them away. Either that or have a yard sale for the benefit of wayward virgins."

"You'll need somebody else to carry your message—like someone who might know where to find your husband."

"Oh, come now. Let us not be Victorian."

"I haven't seen Mr. Douglas since last night when I left him on the beach at his own suggestion to wait with Officer Bean's body till the State Troopers came. He didn't wait."

She laughed.

"Of course, he wouldn't. On a cold beach with a cold corpse when just up above there was a warm house and a warm bed and a warm bedfellow."

"Anybody ever tell you that you are a stupid woman with a dirty mouth?"

"Anybody ever tell you you're a silly prig?"

"Mrs. Douglas," I said, "if this is your way of checking up on your husband, you can satisfy yourself that you have drawn a blank. When he left the beach last night, he didn't come up to the house, not even to do the minimally decent thing and tell me that he was leaving. The first I knew that he was not down there with Bean's body was when I went down and found the body alone. You'll have to go somewhere else to look for your husband."

While I was saying that, the postmistress finished the mail distribution and rolled up the screen that had been shutting off her window. It went up with a loud rattle. I was standing right by Sam's box. Turning away from the gaudy bitch, I unlocked it and pulled out the mail. It gave me something to do with my hands. They needed something to busy them because they very much wanted to slap Mrs. Creighton Douglas on her ugly, pink mouth.

I slammed the box shut. When I turned away from it, I didn't come back face to face with the virago. She had moved on down the line and was pulling the letters out of her own box.

Mathilda was right at my feet and together we started for the door. Just then it swung open and two young guys came in. I didn't need the reaction of the assembled citizenry to give me a line on who they were. They had the look. They were burly, but in proportion to the rest of their bodies they were big bottomed.

Spend too much of your time sitting and the spread is inevitable. It makes little difference what you sit on. A motorcycle saddle will do it. They had the stains of motor grease on their jeans and their T-shirts and the black rims to their fingernails. Their long hair hung in greasy clumps. In adding up the sums for and against the motorcycle boys, Boudreau hadn't mentioned their dirty hair and, on second thought, I decided it didn't have to mean anything. A salt-water swim, if not followed by a shower, isn't much good as a shampoo.

The people, as though with one mind among them, edged away from the two oafs. One of the two scowled, but the other one laughed. They went through to one of the boxes and pulled out the mail. Their path to the door lay open except for Erridge and his dog. We were only just clear of the doorway when they came through. Hit with one of her spells of bad judgment, Mathilda made overtures. It was a tail-wagging jump at the one with the scowl. Snarling at her, he kicked her.

Jumping between them, I grabbed a handful of greasy shirt. I didn't want Mathilda grabbing a mouthful of dirty ankle. It could have poisoned the pup. Putting everything I had into it, I rocked the lout's head with a couple of quick slaps and then shoved him into the arms of the other kid.

"Take him away from here," I said, "before I beat the hell out of him."

I won't pretend that all of that was for the young oaf. A lot of what I had held back when I'd been face to face with Marian Douglas I unloaded on him. I didn't wait around to see them move out. I had to get Mathilda away from them. Their ankles were still in jeopardy. My concern, however, was for Mathilda's digestion.

We walked around to the doctor's office. The time for his office hours had struck. I had planned to leave Mathilda to wait for me in the Porsche but, now that there had come up the possibility of her getting involved in some undesirable entanglement during my absence, I took her into the doctor's office with me.

We were kept waiting. It was evident that the sick took precedence over the merely conversational, but the waiting time wasn't wasted. The receptionist, who had begun by being friendly and had then done a quick cooling down, was now warming to us again. That, of course, was Mathilda's doing. First time around I hadn't brought her in with me. When all the patients had been taken care of, we were ushered in to talk to the doctor. It hadn't been as long a wait as that might sound. I had, as a matter of fact, begun to think that Dr. Buller didn't have much of a practice.

I later learned different. There weren't many that came to see him but that was only because all too many required or demanded that he make house calls. It's likely to be that way in a place where people go for retirement. There will be the people like Sam who can no longer make it to the office, but there will also be the people who are just too imperious to go to anyone. Everyone must come to them.

Dr. Buller was a young guy. Knowing Sam, I had expected that his doctor would be. Sam believed in youth and he believed in scientific progress. In Sam's way of thinking, it therefore followed that the later a man had gone through medical school, the more likely he would be to be up on the newest medical developments. If you talk to Sam about experience and maturity, he would tell you that maturity for most people was a process of for-

getting what they should have remembered and that, also
for most people, experience did nothing but dull the fine
edge of the mind.

The doctor was big and husky. He had one of those
pleasantly ugly faces that will make you trust a man on
sight—like an amiable and even-tempered big bulldog.
He had the handshake that went with it. Firm and
strong, it told you that he could hand you a bone crusher.
He didn't because he was the kind of guy that would control it.

"The general has spoken of you, Mr. Erridge," he said.
"You're his boy."

"He's been something like a father," I said, "and very
much a friend."

"My nurse tells me you have something to tell me,
something you think I should know."

"You have Sam on a lot of medication. He isn't taking
any of it."

The doctor grinned. Mathilda, of course, was busily
making up to him. Since he was bent over to give her the
kind of roughing up that she enjoys and that she expects
from her friends, I had no way of knowing whether he
was grinning at the pup or at this news I was bringing
him.

"It's okay," he said, "but we're not telling anybody."

"You knew?"

"The things I prescribed for him produce certain recognizable effects. These will show up with a difference of
degree from patient to patient, but to some degree they
will show up in any patient. In the general's case, they
don't occur to any degree. I've drawn the obvious conclusions. I've looked into his wastepaper basket and verified
the conclusions."

"Doesn't it matter?"

"Since he's as happy without them, I'd say he's doing well and it doesn't matter."

"He's doing well then?" I said. "I thought not."

"In what way, sir?" the doctor asked.

"He seems to grow feebler by the hour," I said. "I would have said he's dying."

"He is, but so are all the rest of us. Since he is older, he is closer to it. You are quite right in thinking he is very close. In this respect we are like machines, Mr. Erridge. We also have our built-in obsolescence. Use our bodies long enough and they begin to wear out. After a long time the wear becomes general and irreparable. Our friend, General Sam, has had a long time and he's made good use of it. Now he's coming to the end. If doing well is to mean renewed vigor, a new lease on life, we can't hope for that. Now, doing well means that he will finish it as comfortably and as happily as we can manage for him."

"I can understand that, but I can't understand about the medicines."

"Yes, the pills and capsules. Patients in his condition may sleep a little better if they take them. In their waking times they may be in better spirits. That can be true for patients who want them. General Sam is a patient who doesn't want them. To take them would make him feel diminished. He's a man who has always depended on himself. To be dependent on pharmaceutical assistance would depress him. By rejecting the medications, he feels that at least to that extent he is still his own man. It's a feeling that is important to him and having that feeling is doing him more good than anything he could have from the medicines. That's the best we can do for him, Mr. Erridge, helping him to come to the end without too much loss of self-esteem."

"I can buy that," I said. "I can buy it because I know Sam Dalton, but why then do you go on giving him all this stuff since you know he's throwing it away?"

"I go on giving it to him because I have been careful that he shouldn't know that I know. He thinks he is putting one over on me and thinking that does much toward making him feel he is still his own man. It's a game we play and he's winning. Believe me, I would rather it could be that he was beating me at tennis as he did not too many years ago. This is a small triumph, but unhappily he is down to small triumphs. I'm not going to spoil it by giving him the idea that he's winning only because I'm letting him win."

"Then why aren't you just prescribing placebos, or is that what you are doing?"

"Since it is doing no harm, Mr. Erridge, allow me to be that much irrational. With another patient I would probably substitute placebos, but not with General Sam. I'm his physician but I am also his friend. As his friend, I want his little triumph to be as far as possible genuine. I wouldn't like the thought that I was putting one over on him."

I got up to go.

"Okay, Doctor. I'll keep my mouth shut and I'll play along. I appreciate your talking to me."

I offered him my hand, but he wasn't quite ready to take it.

"It's not only saying nothing to General Sam. It's nothing to anybody. His man knows, of course, but he takes his orders from me and he's playing along. I had to go into it with him because I didn't want him standing over the general to watch him take the stuff. Also, since he empties the wastepaper basket, there was always the chance that he would notice that it wasn't only paper he was emptying out of it. Actually it's important that he's the one who always takes care of emptying it. It keeps anyone else from knowing. And now that I think of it, how did you know?"

I would have preferred that he had not asked that question. I couldn't help wincing as I answered it.

"An old friend, his boy, Sam trusted me. He let me see him dump the stuff. So that's what it comes to. I'm betraying him."

"Not in any way that matters," Buller said. "The one to whom he must not be betrayed is Millie. She's a great girl and she's crazy about her granddad, as well she might be, but she'll never understand the way General Sam feels about himself and how important that feeling is to him. Wanting everything done for him that can be done, she'll make him and herself miserable about it. Either she'll keep at him till he breaks down and takes the stuff and that will make him unhappy, or he'll stand fast and she'll be miserable. She isn't happy about him in any case, she hardly could be, but at least she hasn't any doubt that there's been no stone left unturned. If she begins to doubt . . ."

"I've known her all her life," I said. "You couldn't be more right about her."

We shook on that and Mathilda and I turned to leave. The doctor walked out with us. He was going around to Main Street to grab himself some lunch. It's no town for restaurants. There's the one place. It gets by on its bar business. In the food department I'd always thought it was limited only to strangers and even those only the once. It's the kind of place where the chowder will never

come to you hot enough unless there's a feud going between the cook and the waiter. Carried by that waiter,
properly hot chowder would scald his thumb.

"You eat there often?" I asked.

"Only when I haven't the time to fix something for myself," he said. Then listening to his own words, he ap-
pended a quick afterthought. "Or like today when I'm
feeling lazy," he said.

"You aren't feeling lazy," I said. "You've let me cut into
your lunch break."

He laughed.

"Nothing of the kind," he said. "If I hadn't been too
lazy for it, we could have talked out in the kitchen while
I was hotting something up for myself."

As soon as we had come out onto the Common, I had
seen it. He hadn't and it wasn't too astonishing that he
wouldn't. He was in a hurry and she wasn't his. I had a
fine lot of cursing to do but I was holding back on it. I
was working at showing nothing until after he had
jumped into his car and rolled off toward Main Street.

It was Baby. She was sitting where I had parked her
but not at all as I had parked her. All four of her tires
were flat. I had only the one question in my mind. Had
the tires been slashed or was it only that the valve caps
had been loosened and the air let out?

I examined the tires. They were intact. It was just
going to be the job of pumping them back up again. I had
a hand pump in the trunk but, before I brought it out, I
had my cursing to do. For a couple of moments I just
stood there and did it. Mathilda sniffed at the tire valves
and did her own. Whether it was only that she caught
the mood from me or something she was recognizing in
the scent she was picking up from Baby's wheels, I have
no way of knowing.

There was a folded piece of grubby paper tucked into the windshield. It was just where a parking ticket would have been left, but I had every reason for knowing that it wasn't a parking ticket. There was no restriction on parking around the Common. There has never been a policeman with hands so dirty that he leaves black fingermarks on the tickets he issues. Also that day the town had no policeman to be issuing tickets. Even Beebee Bean's stop-sign specialty was being neglected. Beebee was dead.

I took it off the windshield and unfolded it. The message could not have been clearer.

"Up yours, hard guy."

I brought out the hand pump and went to work. I didn't do the complete job that would have brought the rubber up to optimum pressure. I gave the tires only enough air to make it possible for me to roll on them the couple of hundred yards that would take me to the garage by the golf links without slicing the tires or damaging the rims. They were too squishy and sloppy to let Baby handle properly, but by creeping along and asking only the minimum of her, I got it made. At the garage it was no problem to bring them up to where they should have been. Orville, the garageman, knows Baby. Ever since the first time I brought her to those parts, he's been one of her admirers. When I rolled her in on four floppy shoes, he couldn't not take notice of it.

"Somebody been messing around with her?" he asked.

"A couple of young slobs," I said.

While the air was pouring in, I added a quick description of the pair of louts. Orville grimaced. He looked as though he was smelling something bad. Obviously my description served. It was the look that pair seemed to bring to people's faces.

"Slow and quick," he said. "Their name is Perkins."

"Slow and quick?"

"Slocum and Amos. Slocum's a year and some older. When he started school, everybody took to calling him Slo, short for Slocum. Then because he was called Slo, it kind of followed along that his brother, Amos, would be called Quick even though, God knows, he never was."

"What do they do?"

"Not much of anything except it's hell-raising. Nothing steady. When they run out of cash for beer and gas, they'll do odd jobs. They do a good, hard day's work when they're working, but it can't ever be for long. A day or two when they need it. For more than that, you couldn't depend on them."

"They'll be part of this motorcycle bunch the whole town's talking about?"

"They ride," Orville said. "They annoy folks, but most times they're not as bad as they're painted. I've known the lot of them all their lives. They do plenty they should get their butts kicked for, like now with your tires. They get the idea somebody's down on them—most everybody's down on them, of course, but when they feel it's somebody in particular—they'll do a thing like that. To get back, you know."

"I know."

"The thing is anything bad it's done around here, right off it's always put on to them. They get blamed for everything and plenty of times it ain't them at all. It'll be some of the summer people's kids."

"Last night," I said.

"Old Beebee. Not them, not in a million years. I know everybody's thinking it's them, but it isn't. Matter of fact, that's how Beebee come to get killed."

"How?" I asked.

"He gets a call that time of night. It's crazy hell-raising down on the beach. It's laughing and hooting and hollering, keeping folks awake. So what's Beebee going to think? He thinks it's going to be like always—Slo and Quick and them others, Whitey and Clem and Hobie. He'll just go over there and eat them out and they'll simmer down. He's done it so many times, he's got no call to think it's going to be any different this time. So he walks right into it, bringing nothing with him but his mouth. He has no reason to be careful, no reason for going in with his guard up, except that this time it isn't them."

"Summer people's kids?" I asked.

Orville was quick to back away from that.

"I'm not accusing anybody," he said. "We never had anything like this around here before—shooting, killing, we've never had it. So who can say it's like this one or like that one? It's not like anybody I know around here and that goes for the five of them, too. It's just not like them. They don't carry guns. They don't kill."

"There's always a first time," I said. "There can always be just the once. There can't be many people who get to make a career of it."

"Yup," Orville said. "Yup, sure enough, but the first time or just the once, that could be anybody now, couldn't it?"

I agreed that it could. By that time Baby was properly shod again and we pulled away from the garage. Driving back to the house for lunch, I was thinking that what Orville had been saying was not without sense. There was, however, one aspect that he was ignoring. Part of the night's events had been in character for Slo and Quick and their buddies. Two things were out of character for them—the shooting and the way the guys had come to the beach and gone from it. They hadn't been on motorcycles. There had been a boat. The rest of it, however, had been all too much in character, so much in character, in fact, that Orville was saying it was just the thing that had led Beebee Bean to his death.

I could see two ways one could take that. It could mean that it was the five, and they had simply gone from bad to worse. I couldn't like that one much. It smacked too strongly of the kind of glib thinking that says that little misdemeanors inevitably lead to a life of major crime. I've known too many guys who throughout boyhood were constantly told that they had been born to be hanged and then they grew up to be solid citizens, pillars of society. The other way, however, was elaborate; but, more than that, all the evidence seemed to be running against it.

Somebody is out to get Beebee Bean. He builds all that crazy nonsense on the beach just to suck Bean into thinking he'll be coming up against nothing formidable, just those five oafs making a nuisance of themselves again. He gets Beebee to the beach where he can knock him off. I had no sooner thought that one up before I was attacking it from every angle and knocking it down.

It hadn't been just one person on the beach. It hadn't been just one voice. It had been a babble of voices. That would mean a gang attack on the town cop or one attacker working with a number of confederates. That in itself made the thing look shaky. Bean had been a bland and comic character. Nobody was suggesting that he had ever had an enemy in this world or that there could have been anyone who would have made a plan to do away with him.

So it was a puzzle, but it wasn't my puzzle. It belonged to the State Troopers and to the townspeople. I wasn't a resident. I wasn't a taxpayer. I was just a visitor, just a guy passing through.

Back at the house Sam had had his lunch and was taking an afternoon nap. I apologized to Clara for my lateness, but she said I wasn't late at all. Millie had only just gotten up. She was out in the garden with Mrs. Ainsley. Mrs. Ainsley had stopped by and they were having a sherry. If I would join them, there were snacks out there with the sherry. Clara was hoping the snacks might stay me till Mrs. Ainsley would go home to her own lunch and Clara could give us ours.

I knew Martha Ainsley from previous visits I'd made to Sam. Hers was the house next door, but along their road next door didn't have anybody rubbing elbows. The houses had large stretches of lawn and gardens to each side of them, and lawn was separated from lawn and garden from garden by an all but impenetrable band that had been left with its wild growth untouched. Oaks, maples, birches, and spruce rose out of a head-high tangle of vines and brambles. To visit from house to house, you went by the road. To cut yourself a way of more direct access, you would have needed a machete.

There is the road, however, and along the road people do visit. Local custom has always called for sherry at noon and cocktails at five. Mrs. Ainsley, furthermore, had always been the solid rock on which was founded local custom. She had reached that age at which a woman turns to counting her years as ornaments. She makes no attempt to conceal them or to minimize them. She boasts about them. She flaunts them. She was by a few years Sam's junior, but not by so many that she hadn't danced with him at West Point hops.

She walked with a stick, but she had been carrying it for years. It had never seemed to me that she leaned on it or used it to steady herself. There had been the times when I had had the occasion to offer her my arm and she had taken it, but she had only taken it. She had never rested so much as an ounce of weight on it. She would take it only as a token of the deference properly due to a widow of her standing. Similarly, I was convinced, she carried the stick only as a badge of authority. With only a little more grandeur she might have been followed about by a standard bearer to carry it for her.

She was tall and she was straight-backed. She carried her head high. She was a native. It had been through her that Sam had come to know the bay. She was convinced that it had been to be near her that he had chosen to go there in his retirement. He was fond of her and she was devoted to him. I knew that. She was widely known as a terror, but she had never terrorized me. From our first meeting I had been granted a special place because I was Sam's boy. Her greeting now was a command.

"Matthew," she said. "Come and tell me I had reason for what I did last night. I killed that fat fool."

CHAPTER 5

Indirectly perhaps. In a manner of speaking, maybe yes.

It was she who had called Beebee Bean. She had dispatched him to the beach to still that unseemly uproar. She was now ordering me to speak, but as was her way, she wasn't pausing long enough to allow me to put a word in. I just listened while I poured myself a Tio Pepe and attacked Clara's snacks. They were native crab meat piled on rounds of toast, strips of dried salt herring, and, out of the garden, baby carrots, tiny radishes, little blue-nosed turnips, and infant leeks.

"You know how I am," she was saying. "For all my years, my hearing is sharp and I still read the smallest print without glasses. I have all my faculties unimpaired. Last night I was cursed with them."

"The noise woke you," I said.

"For me it didn't matter," she said. "If one thing doesn't wake me, another thing does. I'm an old woman, but I'm not a complaining old biddy. I've been telling myself that all morning. I'd have done nothing about it if I hadn't been concerned for Sam, and now Millie tells me that he slept right through it. I can't say I'm not glad that he slept through it, but I also cannot say I'm not sorry. I killed that fat idiot needlessly."

"Just because you called him?" Millie said. "Nobody could have dreamed there'd be shooting. Matt was on his way down to the beach to deal with them. If it hadn't been Bean, it could have been Matt."

"But I didn't only call him, Millie. I told him it was those stupid boys down there. How could he have dreamed that he would be going into danger when I'd told him that?"

"You saw the boys?" I asked.

"Matthew, that's silly. How could I have seen them? Do you imagine that I would have gone out in the cold, wading through the dew in my nightdress? If I had been up and dressed, of course, I would have gone down and told them what for myself, but in my nightdress, Matthew?"

She hadn't seen them but she had heard them. She knew their voices. She couldn't say that she had recognized each of the five voices individually, but she could speak for Slo and Quick and Clem.

"The five are always together," she said. "They've always done their devilment in a group and there were more than the three voices, so it follows that Hobart and Joshua would also have been there."

"Hobie," I said. "Is Joshua the one they call Whitey?"

"That's the five of them, the young demons."

"Have you talked to the State Troopers?" I asked.

"They came to see me this morning," she said. "They knew that I'd made the call to Bean. They'd learned that much from Sharon."

"Sharon will be the telephone operator?"

"Yes, and there's never been a sillier young woman, but she comes by it naturally. It's in the genes. Her mother was a fool. I can remember when the child was born and I first heard that she was calling it Sharon, an absurd name."

I refrained from saying that was beside the point. To get her back on the track, I tried a question instead.

"Did you tell the troopers that you recognized the voices?" I asked.

She fixed me with a withering look.

"I'm an old woman, Matthew," she said, "but I haven't come to such a pass that I babble."

"You don't think you ought to tell them?"

"Most certainly not. Haven't I already done more than enough damage? I sent Burton Bean to his death. I will not have those stupid lads on my conscience as well."

It was a statement of resolution. I knew how Martha Ainsley was wont to choose her words. She was inflexible in the distinction she made between "shall" and "will." She had spoken, and the woman had a will of steel.

"Your duty as a citizen," I said.

"It is my duty as a citizen to see that my garbage is put out for collection properly packaged so that the animals can't get at it and strew it over the road. It is my duty as a citizen to pay my taxes and to cast my vote. It is my duty as a citizen to speak out in town meeting against all the insanities that may be proposed. It is not my duty as a citizen to be an informer."

"There's a great space between not withholding from the authorities knowledge of a crime and being an informer."

"It would be no good my telling them," she said. "It would only be to make trouble without purpose since I can never swear to what I heard. I don't know that it would be of much evidential value even if I could swear to it, but that doesn't matter since any sort of nonsense might serve to convince a jury and it would inevitably be a jury that would be prejudiced against those stupid lads."

"But as a lead that the troopers should be checking out . . ."

"If I am to be honest with myself," she said, doing a neat reverse on what she had previously been telling me, "I am prejudiced against them myself. I have known

them all their lives. I know their parents. I have been ap-
palled by them. They are stupid. They are brutish. They
have no manners. They are inconsiderate. They are dirty.
They are all of that, but still none of it is reason for accusing them of murder."

"You wouldn't be saying anything about what they are.
You would only be saying what you heard."

"What, being prejudiced against the young demons, I
thought I heard."

I gave up on it. I had to say something to signal my
surrender.

"I'm also prejudiced against them," I said. "At least
against the two brothers, Slo and Quick. One of them
kicked Mathilda this morning and I slapped him around
a little. They got even. They let the air out of my tires."

"Kicking dogs, letting air out of tires, precisely what is
to be expected of them. There's no question but that it
makes them unattractive."

"What if I were to tell the State Troopers?" I asked.

"You would be violating a confidence," she said. "I
shan't go so far as to say it would be enough to make you
unattractive, but let's say less attractive."

She said it with a laugh. I found myself laughing with
her.

"That's a stiff price to pay," I said. "I'll have to think
about it."

"It will be my word against yours," she said. "I have an
unimpeachable reputation for honesty. I'll deny ever having said anything and the whole town knows of your prejudice against the young beasts."

"A prejudice I share with everyone else."

"Yes, but not to the extent of face slapping in the post
office with the whole town looking on."

"I didn't say where and I didn't say before witnesses."

"You can't have thought I wouldn't have heard," she said. "You know the town better than that."

That there was a gossip network and that it operated with impressive speed and efficiency I had, of course, known. Faced with this demonstration of it, my mind jumped to that other item of the morning's doings in the post office. If my encounter with Slo and Quick had already done the rounds, could that far juicier bit have been far behind? I said nothing, but involuntarily I darted a glance at Millie. It was too transparent. I gave myself away.

Millie laughed.

"Don't take it so hard, darling," she said. "It was only the most recent of a series of messages. They come regularly."

"Does Sam know?" I asked.

"Oh, come! Please, Matt, keep Sam out of this."

Reaching out with her stick, Martha Ainsley rapped me smartly on the shin.

"Sam doesn't know and you're not going to breathe a word of this to him," she said. "If you feel you must tell the State Troopers that I recognized those voices, that will be a compulsion I can bring myself to understand, but to speak to Sam about this vile harridan's ugly nonsense will be unforgivable."

"At least unforgivable," I said, "not to speak of hard on my shins. What's eating on me is that there are people who do the unforgivable, people who even make a career of it—the Douglas bitch herself, for example."

Jointly they reassured me. Sam was seeing few people and those were only the people he chose to see. Marian Douglas was most emphatically not one of them.

"We've never liked the woman, Sam and I," Mrs. Ainsley said. "Neither of us has ever made a secret of our feelings. To be honest about it, there has been no love lost either way. Now, of course, there is also the woman's terror of death. It's one of her many vulgarities. She was an only child. That didn't stop her spending the whole year of her mother's last illness abroad, leaving the poor woman to be cared for by unsupervised strangers. She was careful not to come home until after the funeral."

They gave me every assurance that among the few people Sam was seeing there was none who would ever say anything that might upset him.

"Dexter?"

"Dexter," Millie said, "knows where his bread is buttered."

"And he butters it on both sides," said Martha Ainsley, as she rose to leave.

Millie and I went in to lunch and I asked her if she knew what that parting crack meant.

"Marian Douglas, she's taken up with Dexter," Millie said. "He goes to her on his nights off."

"And on Dexter's nights off, Douglas comes here?"

Millie laughed.

"Came, Matt darling, came. It's like a wife swap, isn't it. Except that I'm not anybody's wife," she said.

It was obvious that she was waiting for me to say something to that. She was expecting something middle-aged. I sidestepped it.

"And still you're certain he won't be carrying her messages?" I asked instead.

"He hasn't and he won't. The fool thinks they are a secret. He thinks nobody knows about them."

"Obviously there's talk. How can he not know?"

"You know this place. There are the people who belong

and the people who don't belong. You have to belong if you are going to hear what goes around. Dexter doesn't belong."

"Since that performance Marian Douglas put on this morning is nothing new and since you haven't been letting it bother you, why did Martha have to come hurrying over to tell you about it?"

"She always hurries to tell me. She keeps hoping it will get to me and I'll stop seeing him."

"I've known worse ideas."

"Have you? Then be happy. I'm not going to be seeing him anymore. I was thinking last night that it might be time to put a stop to it. Now it seems it is the time."

"Why now? Or is it none of my business?"

"It is none of your business, but there's no reason why I shouldn't tell you anyhow. Last night he kept telling me that he was going to leave her. I didn't really believe him but, since he didn't go home last night, it looks as though he has done it. If he has, that'll be it. I won't have him coming over here anymore."

"Because if it's no longer husband snatching, the fun will have gone out of it?"

"Is that meant to hurt, Matt?"

"A spanking that doesn't hurt is a waste of time."

"Then you're wasting your time. There isn't much around here in the way of diversion. Creighton Douglas is amusing. There isn't anyone else around here who'll give me the time. Dexter? After all, since I've been spelling him for his time off, he wasn't any good for going places with."

That was too much. I exploded.

"Dexter," I said. "That couldn't be the only reason why he wouldn't do?"

She laughed.

"Obviously it couldn't," she said. "All he wants from a woman is wide-eyed worship of his male beauty. If there's any beautiful-body worship going, it has to be my beautiful female body."

I couldn't see how she could ever have had as much as a thought of him. I said as much.

"Look around you," she said. "Up here there's so little going that a girl scrapes the bottom of the barrel. Swains of more suitable age? You met a couple of those in the post office this morning. A bit young maybe, but it's them or it's the semidetached older man. The semidetached older man is not only something better than a cretin. He also takes showers. On that alone he has a great deal going for him."

"But now that he has detached himself?"

"Only to re-enter the marriage market. The quicker I take myself out of that sort of deal, the better."

"Had you given him any reason to expect . . . ?"

"Did I lead him on to the place where he would leave his wife for me? The answer is no, I didn't. Crate Douglas forms his own expectations. Last night he gave me a glimpse of the way his mind works and I told him to forget it. Now it looks as if telling him wasn't enough. He's left her in spite of everything I said. So now I'm not going to see him again. As soon as he'll be convinced of that, he'll be going back to her. You must understand that for Creighton Douglas it's not her or me. It's her money or my money. When he marries, he doesn't take a wife. He takes his wife's financial holdings. I'm not buying."

"The money is hers?"

"Why do you think he married her? Why do you think he's stayed with her?"

"In that case, I should think she would have been keeping him on a shorter leash."

"Not when it served her purpose to let him roam. He's been her defense against Dexter and others before Dexter."

She was off on a tack I couldn't follow.

"Defense?" I asked.

"Yes. No problems about having Dexter for fun in bed. Since she has a husband, Dexter is stopped from working on any ideas of getting himself a rich wife. It allows him only to have those ideas and they keep him dancing attendance. If she rids herself of Crate, she'll have no way of holding a Dexter short of marrying one. As long as she keeps Crate, she can dangle Dexter."

"Great people you've mixed yourself up with," I said.

"Now, look," she said. "You can't blame Dexter on me. I found him already installed when I first got here. Dexter was Jerry Buller's choice. Creighton Douglas? I've been having a dull time and he was about all that was available. He was good company and his wife was otherwise occupied. I thought he would be all right for amusement, just for want of anything else. All right, so now I know better."

"He asked you to marry him last night?"

"After his fashion."

"And what was that?"

"It was nasty. It was money. I hate money talk."

She had been trying to keep it to herself, but once she was started, it poured out of her. She seemed to find some relief in unloading it onto me. Douglas had talked around marriage. There had been a lot of stuff about the wrong time. With Sam so sick, of course, they couldn't, but he wanted Millie to be thinking about it for afterward.

She didn't have to say much about the money angle. I knew her financial setup and I knew Sam's. I could fill in the details for myself. She had lost both her parents when she was a baby. Sam and Mrs. Sam had brought her up and for most of her teens it had been Sam alone. The money her parents had left hadn't been any staggering fortune, but it hadn't been a pittance either. Also under Sam's management it had come in for some healthy growth. She was a well-heeled young woman. Since she was all the family Sam had left and since Sam was the most doting of grandfathers, she would on his death be having his money as well, and Sam was a rich man.

The guy's pitch had been that he knew how it was between her grandfather and her. He wouldn't dream of taking her away as long as the old man needed her, but afterward they would go off together. He would get a divorce and they would marry.

"I told him to forget it," Millie said. "I told him it would never happen. I didn't love him. I even told him that, just through his talking about it, I was coming to the place where I didn't even like him. I told him that, if he was getting those ideas, it would be better if we didn't see each other anymore. You can see what kind of a game he was playing, Matt."

I could see and I was glad that she could. The guy knew full well that Sam had no use for him. He wanted to play it cozy until Sam would be gone. He wasn't taking any risk of Sam cutting her out of his will. Douglas could go on sitting pretty with his wife's money until he could make the switch and do it without any financial loss.

"When he realized last night that you were seeing through him," I said, "he changed his tactics."

"That's it, Matt. He thinks he can get me to believe that I had him wrong. He's left her. He hasn't waited.

He's trying to force my hand. I was thinking the time had come for me to stop seeing him. Now I know it has."

"You're going to be bored," I said.

She laughed.

"With you around?" she said. "Don't be silly."

Sam woke from his nap and we went in to sit with him. He didn't ask me whether I had talked to the doctor, but with Millie around he obviously wasn't going to ask. Dexter was around as well and more than ever he seemed to be on Sam's nerves. When he began hinting that if I wasn't planning on anything that evening, perhaps he could have some extra time off, Millie started blowing up; but, as it began coming through to her that Sam was ready to jump at the chance of having another evening free of Dexter, she subsided. It was settled that Dexter could take off. Then, when evening had come around, it was almost unsettled.

Dr. Buller came by to see Sam. He had us out of the room briefly while he was examining his patient, but then we were back in there, just being social around the bed. Buller said something to Millie about saving him a dance, and she said she couldn't since she wasn't going. Sam was quick to pick up on that.

"The golf-club dance," he said. "Since when aren't you going?"

"Since I decided I've been seeing too much of Crate Douglas. I half told him last night that I wouldn't be seeing him anymore. When he comes around tonight, I'm going to finish telling him."

Sam liked that, but his pleasure was something less than complete. She was young, and dancing was for the young. He didn't want her tied down to his bedside. He mumbled about that for a few minutes and then abruptly he brightened.

"Go tonight," he said. "Go with Matt."

"Another time," she said, "when you won't be alone and he asks me."

"He'll ask you and I won't be alone. Dexter will be here."

Dexter, as usual, had been combing his hair. He stowed the comb.

"You gave me the evening off," he said.

"That was before I knew I'd need you tonight."

"But . . ." Dexter began.

"One night off a week," Sam told him. "You had it last night. Extra time has to be at my convenience. Tonight is not convenient."

Dexter subsided but not with good grace. His mutterings were held at that level that lies between the merely audible and the unintelligible. His look was surly. Millie looked troubled. I knew what was eating on her. I was having my own misgivings about the guy's mood. I couldn't be happy about leaving Sam to him. Millie said nothing of that. Giving it the light touch, she went at it from another angle.

"You're being high-handed, Sam. You're handing me around like a parcel. Matt's shown no sign of being suitably eager."

Sam chuckled. He turned to me.

"Come on, young fellow," he said. "Pant a little. Be eager."

At that point the doctor took a hand.

"Only if he beats me to it," he said. "I'm even unsuitably eager. All my patients are stable. There's a good chance I can get through the whole evening without being called away." He looked to Millie. "Okay?"

"I thought you'd never ask," Millie said.

Dexter did everything that needed to be done for Sam

before he left. In all justice to the man, he scanted nothing even though he did break all records for speed and efficiency. He obviously wanted to be out and away before there could be another change in plans.

There was no change. Dexter prettied himself up and took off. Sam wanted to get up for dinner. He made it to the table with my help. Millie had changed for the dance and I could see that she had put a lot more effort into it than she had the night before. In any case the kid was radiant, and both she and Sam were in high good spirits. We were having our coffee before either of them spoke of Creighton Douglas. Millie looked at the time.

"Either I was more convincing last night than I thought or the man has been having second thoughts. I told him not to come around tonight, but he said he would come anyway. He was expecting me to change my mind."

"If he turns up after you've gone," Sam said, "we'll take care of kicking him out, Matt and I. I'll tell him and Matt will do the punting."

"None of that," Millie said. "Just tell him I'm out."

"You don't want him thinking he can go over to the club and pick up with you there," Sam said.

"He won't think that. He'll get the message. He'll know that I meant what I said last night."

"He's got a thick skin and a thick head."

"Darling, stop worrying. He's nothing I can't handle and, if I should be wrong about that, remember I'll be with Jerry. You may think Jerry isn't as tough as Matt and you, but he's no kitten."

Buller came around and picked her up. Under Sam's all too transparent God-bless-you-my-children look, they took off.

"That's a good boy," Sam said. "I used to wish you

were like ten or fifteen years younger, but Jerry Buller's okay."

"Matchmaking, Sam?"

"In collusion with Millie. She likes the boy. He needs to be pushed. I'd like to see her settled, Matt. There have been too many lightweights and then Douglas. He's been the worst of the lot, a middle-aged lightweight, for God's sake. Of course, she's never taken any of them seriously, but it's time there was a real man. It's for both of them. Jerry's what she needs and she's what he needs."

"I like your Dr. Buller," I said.

Sam studied me for a moment.

"Just on sight?" he said.

"I make snap judgments," I said. "Just on sight I didn't take to Douglas."

"The Crate? He was too easy," Sam said. "I was thinking that you might have had a long talk with Jerry, telling him that he has an insubordinate patient."

I didn't like lying to Sam.

"I'm still thinking about it," I said.

That was true enough. My talk with Jerry Buller was very much on my mind.

Sam and I spent the evening much as we had the one before. He beat me at chess. We talked. He ran out of energy and fell asleep. I watched the ball game on the tube and when it was over, I found myself something to read.

When it came, it was earlier than it had been the previous night. Otherwise it was much the same as it had been. There were differences, but they seemed minor. Again it was sounds of revelry by night—voices and laughter. The sounds fell far short of being as loud as they had been the previous time. They were well below the level where they could be pulling anyone out of sleep. I was hearing them, but I was awake and I was only just hearing them.

There was also another difference. This time they were not coming at me from the beach down below the garden and the lawn. They were coming from the other side of the house, from the direction of the driveway and the road.

Ordinarily I might have given it not much thought and I might not have been impelled to go out and do anything about it. This, however, was not ordinarily. Just on the basis of what had happened the night before it was nothing that could be ignored, but there was another factor as well. Baby was out there parked in the driveway and Baby had been the morning's target. I could well imagine that it had been with just such joking and laughter that they had gone about the job of letting the air out of the Porsche's tires.

The least I could do was get myself out there to knock some dirty heads together. I started up, but I hadn't made it even halfway to the door before I was having second thoughts. Hadn't Beebee Bean gone to the beach with just some such course of action in mind?

Sam had a .45 and I knew where he'd always kept it. It had always been in his study, in the drawer of his desk. I wasn't having any ideas of shooting anybody. My mind was running more in the direction of a warning shot. The study was where I had been with my book. I turned back and tried the desk drawer. It wasn't locked, but the .45 wasn't there. I tried the other drawers, but with no more success.

I was beginning to feel sick—kicked-in-the-gut sick. I wanted to think I was wrong, but now I had to know. My need for the gun was no longer important. I went into

Sam's room. He was sleeping soundly. I tried the drawer of his bedside table. The .45 was there. My fingers closed over the barrel. I stood there for a moment with the gun in my hand, trying to think and getting nowhere with it.

I shut the drawer and tiptoed out of the room. The light was on in the hall. If I opened the door and went out that way, I would be silhouetted in the lighted doorway. I had a better idea. The kitchen was dark. Going by the kitchen door, I could slip out unseen. I could even do better than that. There was a light mounted on the garage for floodlighting the driveway. The switch was in the kitchen. It would be like sending up flares to light the battleground before moving to the attack.

I fumbled around in the dark kitchen trying to locate the floodlight switch. I had no luck with it, and I didn't want to turn on the kitchen light. That would have given me away. I remembered that a good flash was always kept on the shelf beside the kitchen door. Even in the dark I had no trouble laying my hand on that. It was going to do.

I slipped out the kitchen door. Guiding on the voices and the laughter, I could sneak up on the trespassers in the dark. I was telling myself that I also had something else to guide on. Those guys were out there having fun and games and it was a cinch that they were having their fun and games with the Porsche. I knew the precise spot where I had left her. I could just head toward Baby.

I had the flashlight but I was holding back on that until I would be all but on them. My tactics might have been good. I'll never know because I didn't get to carry through on them. There was the one factor I should never have forgotten, and I had allowed it to slip my mind. The jolt of discovering that Sam had been keeping his .45 in the drawer of his bedside table and the implications of his having it there had been too powerful. It had taken my eye off the ball.

I had forgotten Mathilda. All the time I had been moving through unlighted rooms and fumbling around in the dark kitchen, she must have been right there with me. Any other time I would have been aware of her, or at least I would have had it in mind to leave her shut up in the house when I went out.

The first I knew that she had been with me and that with me she had slipped out of the house was when I heard the snarl quickly followed by a scream. I could think of nothing but that the pup was about to be shot. Flicking on the flashlight, I took off toward her. It was only for a moment that I had her in the light, Mathilda with a tenaciously held mouthful of jeans and ankle. In that single moment I saw the pup. I saw the leg into which she had fastened her teeth. I saw a motorcycle. I saw the Porsche with a length of hose hanging out of its gas tank.

I had no time for piecing all these details together into any coherent picture. Out of the dark everything came at me at once. A glancing blow grazed my left ear. It was no credit to me that it didn't land squarely. A rolling block that swept my feet out from under me was taking me down just as the punch came at me. I was knocked flat. On a count of arms and legs I knew that there were two guys down there with me, pinning me to the driveway, but they were only part of it. There was another one standing over us. I knew he was there because he spoke and his voice came from overhead. Light also came at me from up there.

I still had the .45 in my hand, but with my arms pinned to the ground it was useless. I didn't have it for long. The instant the light fell on it, a heel ground into the wrist of my gun hand. The .45 dropped out of my grasp.

It was about then that Mathilda started barking. It was her rage-and-frustration barking. It had to mean that she had been broken loose from her mouthful of ankle and was now under restraint. I saw a hand dart down and grab up the gun. I don't know why I didn't think that I might be shot. I was certain that Mathilda would be the target. No shot came, only a thud. I was guessing that the .45 had been thrown aside but, even while I was making the guess, I was asking myself whether it mightn't be wishful thinking.

Now there were two voices coming at me from above. The one who had spoken before asked the question.

"That your man?"

"That's him."

The first voice snapped out orders.

"Pick him up, you guys, and hang on to him. Don't forget this is Mr. Hard Guy and he ain't been softened up yet."

I was jerked to my feet with my arms pinned behind me.

"Okay, boy," the first voice said. "Take him. He's yours."

CHAPTER 6

I did what I could. I flailed around and I kicked some shins, but that was the limit of what I could manage. The two who were holding me had me firmly pinioned and there was no light but the single beam that was trained on me. It showed me nothing. It had me blinded. Apart from Mathilda's enraged barking, everything had dropped into ominous silence. There was no more of even the subdued hooting and laughter.

There were only the slaps. It may well have been that the sound of them was not as sharp or as loud as pistol shots. Since they were rocking my head back and forth, in my ears they were fully that loud. I could read them for what they were. This would be the oaf I had slapped. He was now getting his own back. More than that, he was collecting interest. There was only one question: Just how usurious would the transaction be?

The question remained unanswered. The whole of the driveway was suddenly flooded with light. Someone had gone into the kitchen and hit that switch I hadn't been able to locate. I could only think it was Dexter, back early from his evening's entertainment. He had come in some time while I'd been reading and hadn't bothered to let me know he was in the house. It could have been. After all, he had let me pull duty for him through the whole of the night before.

So, I was thinking, Dexter had been lagging it, but I

wasn't giving the thought much time. It was of no immediate importance. I was waiting for him to come out and
do what he could toward evening the odds, but nobody
came. I could well imagine that he might be thinking
that five against two would not be even enough. With the
lot of us out there floodlighted, the count was easy. Playing it cozy, he could have been staying in the house to hit
the phone for State Trooper reinforcements. It would
have been in character. He wouldn't have wanted to get
his hair mussed.

As soon as the light hit, everybody froze. It was only
for a moment, but in that moment I could take in the
tableau. Five guys and two of them I recognized. We had
met that morning. Since the other three were cut to the
same pattern and since there were five motorcycles, the
conclusion was obvious.

Three of them were occupied with me. The remaining
two were up the driveway by the Porsche. One of that
two was fully occupied with keeping his grip on Mathilda's collar. The other was hauling the siphoning hose
out of Baby's gas tank.

After that first instant of surprise, they moved in con-
cert. Nothing was said. The five of them jumped for their
bikes. It was, of course, no simple jump. Two of them had
their hands full of me and a third had his hands full of
Mathilda. The two who were unimpeded had it easy.
They mounted their motorcycles. One of them took over
on the pup's collar. Astride his motorcycle, he kept her
firmly under control. The one who had been her captor
quickly mounted and, lining up alongside his friend, he
also took a grip on Mathilda's collar.

They kicked their motorcycles to life, and I saw them
take off, riding side by side and dragging the dog between them. They could kill her that way and it would

be no easy death. I yelled and I struggled, but I was as
helpless as Mathilda. I was also being dragged. The two
that had hold of me were hauling me up the driveway to
where they had left their motorcycles. For an insane moment I thought they were going to do me as their buddies were doing my poor basset. I was half hoping that
they would. I saw in it the shred of a chance. Surely I
would be able to thrash about between them and make it
enough to wreck them. That I could hardly hope that in
the process I wouldn't be wrecking myself as well seemed
of little concern just then. No matter how strong a guy's
instinct for self-preservation might be, there are those
times when rage takes over. In even the most cautious of
us there lurks that sleeping touch of *kamikaze*.

When it came to it, though, they had other ideas. They
weren't taking me anywhere. They were only making certain that I would be able to do nothing to interfere with
their flight. At the top of the driveway, when we were
close beside the spot where they had left their motorcycles, between them they picked up the whole 190 pounds
of battling Erridge and flung him across the roadside
ditch into a thicket of blackberry bramble.

It was a spot well chosen. I worked at scrambling to
my feet and having at them, but blackberry thorns were
hooked at all points into my clothes and my skin. There
was nothing I could do that was quick. I tried it that way
and I was no time at all learning. Tearing away from one
set of impalings served only to trap me more firmly in another. To free myself from the brambles, I had to work
slowly and methodically. It came close to being a matter
of disengaging myself thorn by thorn, almost one of the
damn things at a time. No few of them, furthermore,
would just spring back and take a fresh hold.

I was still working at it when I heard Mathilda bark. It

was again her angry bark. There was no whine in it and no yelp of pain. It was a heartening sound, and there was something else about it that made it even more heartening. The sound of it was not diminishing in the distance. Mathilda was stationary and she was nearby. The parallel was unmistakable. That pair of lugs hadn't dragged her far. As soon as they had revved up their motorcycles to the place where they could safely let go their hold of her and whiz away from any threat of her teeth, they had turned her loose.

As she limped along the road toward where I was fighting the blackberry tangle, I had the notion that the tone of her barking changed. Now I was hearing in it a sound of urgency. She was telling me it was time I got up out of there and started doing something about the forces of evil. Mathilda won't hold back from fighting her own battles, but through past experience she has come to expect that I will be right in there beside her. It's not that she considers herself dependent on me, but ours is an alliance. It always has been.

I fought my way out of the brambles, and I was only just in time because immediately I had to make a grab at Mathilda's collar and hold the raging basset in check.

The enemy was back, all five of them, but now they were a cowed quintet. They came on foot, walking their motorcycles, and they came under duress. They weren't returning to the fray. They were being herded along the road. I saw them clearly even before they had reached the floodlighted driveway area. They were coming toward me with a car moving slowly up the road behind them. The car's headlights had them silhouetted. The lights also revealed the person who was herding them along. It was Martha Ainsley. She was walking without her stick and she was showing no need of it.

Having once permitted a nightgown to inhibit her from dealing with these oafs, she was not the woman who would make the same mistake twice. She had a quilted bathrobe cinched around her, and she was walking the road in a pair of furry bedroom slippers. The nightgown hung down below the hem of her robe. She was carrying a shotgun and her aim was steady.

For a start she was ignoring Mathilda and me. She was fully occupied with dealing with her captives. Snapping out orders, she positioned them to her satisfaction. At her command, with their hands clasped on their heads they lowered themselves to the driveway, where she had them lie facedown. When they showed a tendency toward spreading out, she was quick to knock that off.

"Close together," she said. "I want all five of you within an area I can cover with the pattern of my shot. It isn't that I couldn't pick you off one by one, but the single blast is easier, more efficient, and more economical."

They mumbled and they whimpered, but they were not taking the risk of crossing her. Pulling together in a tight clump, they arranged themselves on the driveway in the precise pattern she demanded of them. Although she was satisfied, I spotted something she was missing. Sam's .45 was lying on the driveway within too easy reach of the spot where she had placed her prisoners.

Keeping my hold on Mathilda's collar, I jumped for it. As I was coming up with it, Martha, without even for a moment taking her eyes off the recumbent five, snapped her orders at me. She had always been articulate, but now she was articulating out of the corner of her mouth in the best Edward G. Robinson style. The corner of the Robinson mouth, however, had never been so crisp and precise in its enunciation.

"Take your dog inside, Matthew, and shut her away,"

she said. "While you are in there, please ring the State Troopers for me. I shall keep these villains under control until the troopers arrive."

I wanted to suggest that I could take over on the shotgun while she went inside to make the call, but she had a point about Mathilda. I couldn't question the lady's competence in handling the gun. It was doubtful that she cou'd have managed the dog.

Meanwhile the car pulled into the driveway and stopped. It was Buller's car. He was bringing Millie home from the golf-club dance. It wasn't until later that I came around to thinking about the time and realizing that it was considerably after the dance. I did notice the lipstick smudge he would undoubtedly have wiped away before coming into the house. He hadn't expected that he would be floodlighted.

Accepting Millie and Buller as reinforcements, Martha, without a moment's pause and before anyone else could say anything, gave her orders. She had taken command and it was evident that she was not about to relinquish it. This time she snapped the orders out of the other side of her mouth. Now Millie and Buller were the ones delegated to go in and call the troopers.

Millie had yet to learn that hers was not to reason why. She stopped to ask a question.

"What do we tell them?" she said. "What happened?"

"Tell them to get here and fast," Martha Ainsley said.

"Tell them five louts caught stealing gas," I said.

Millie looked me over. She was taking note of my torn shirt, some rents in my pants, and a flock of bleeding scratches.

"And?" she said. "There's more than that."

"They returned to the scene of the crime," Martha said.

"You can tell the troopers that, if you don't mind sounding as though you were on TV."

I could see that Millie had no taste for the duty that had been assigned to her. I could have expected that. The girl has a soft heart. Pity comes easily to her. She can hate the sin but never the sinner. I suppose she was trying to stall, but it wasn't all stalling. There was genuine concern in it, too.

She turned to Buller.

"Jerry," she said, "isn't there something you should be doing for Matt? Look at him. He's bleeding."

"Only scratches," I said. "The bleeding's nothing. There's always more where that comes from."

Buller also had his concern but at that moment his was for Martha Ainsley.

"I'll take the gun," he said, "and you go inside with Millie. You're going to be having a chill."

"I'll be all right. I'm nice and warm," the lady said.

Buller reached for her gun.

"Inside," he said. "Doctor's orders."

With obvious reluctance, she let him take the shotgun out of her hands.

"It's loaded," she said, "and I have the safety off. So watch it, young man."

I took note of that "young man" and I admired it. She was yielding to his authority but not without that small move toward putting him in his place. Taking Millie by the arm, the old lady propelled her toward the house. They took Mathilda off my hands and, between them, they managed her.

Standing over the five louts and holding the shotgun on them, Jerry Buller began ripping them up.

"How dumb can you get?" he said. "The whole town's

working its ass off to pin a murder on you, so you go and work your asses off to beef the thing up for them."

He sounded as though he had a lot more words to lay on them. I could tell that he had no more than begun revving up on it, but he didn't get to say any of them. Since the kitchen door was nearest, the women went in that way. We saw the kitchen light go on and with the light came Millie's scream.

"Jerry," she yelled. "Jerry, quick. It's Sam."

Buller didn't stop to hand the shotgun over to me. He flung it at me even as he was taking off on the run. I caught the gun on the fly. I did it one handed since I was already holding the .45. It wasn't until much later that either of us had the thought that sane men don't play catch with a loaded shotgun, especially when the safety is off. By one of those miracles the thing didn't fire. Neither of us at that moment had been giving much thought to what the thing was. It was just a handful of something neither of us wanted. It was in our way.

I did hang on to it but only to carry it with me as I dashed for that kitchen door, following close on Jerry Buller's heels. Sam was there. Just inside the door he lay on the kitchen floor. Millie was on her knees beside him. Martha was at the kitchen sink. She was running water. I never have known whether she'd been about to dash cold water in Sam's face or had some idea of forcing some between his lips. Buller dropped down beside Millie and began examining Sam. Millie started to her feet. I gave her a hand up. It was all within the moment, but sometime in there I rid myself of the revolver and the shotgun.

I know I had my hands free and I later picked the weapons up off the kitchen floor. It would seem as though I dropped them or tossed them aside, but the odds are that I had the wit to just set them down. Since the shotgun didn't go off, I must have handled it with some care. I have no memory of doing it.

On her feet, Millie grabbed hold of me and hung on. She was shaking badly and strangling on the sobs she was forcing herself to swallow. I put my arms around her and held her. Buller came off his knees and bent to pick Sam up off the floor. Leaving the water running, Martha turned from the sink and, putting her arms around Millie, she took the kid away from me.

Between us, Buller and I picked Sam up and carried him back to his bed. The drawer of his bedside table had been pulled open and left that way. I noticed that and I knew it wasn't the way I had left it. I was completely clear on that bit. After taking the .45 out of the drawer, I had been careful to close it.

Once we had Sam on the bed, I moved off a step or two, putting myself out of Buller's way. He was working on Sam.

"How is he?" I asked.

"Too soon to tell. In the past he's bounced back again and again, but each time there's less resilience left."

"Fainted?"

"More than that. This is stroke."

There wasn't time for anything more to be said before the two women were in the sickroom with us. Millie had pulled herself together. She was white-faced and her eyes were full of pain, but she was steady. She couldn't work up much more than a whisper, but she asked the question.

"Is this it, Jerry?"

"He's alive," Buller said. "He's gone into coma. Now it has to be just wait and see."

That open table drawer was troubling me. I pushed it shut. The women watched me do it. Buller had eyes only for his patient. Mathilda reared up beside me with her forepaws on the edge of the bed. Buller took notice of that.

"Can you get the dog out of here, Millie?" he said.

Millie didn't move.

"You're using her to get me out of here," she said.

Buller snarled at her.

"The last thing I need right now is a mob scene," he said. "People, a dog. General Sam doesn't need that. He needs air."

"Of course," Millie said. "I'm being stupid. Sorry, Jerry."

Without taking his eyes off Sam, he reached for her hand and held it for a few moments. Martha grabbed Mathilda's collar with one hand and fastened on Millie's arm with the other. Firmly she headed them out of the room.

"We'll be standing by for any time when there may be anything we can do," she said, "but, of course, you know that."

"Thank you," Buller said.

I started to move out with them, but he dropped his hand on my shoulder. It was a signal. He wanted me to stay.

"Sam was trying to help me," I said.

"Making it as far as he did was one of those miracles."

"It was more than just making it," I said. "It was from here to his gun case. It was unlocking the case and then all the way out to the kitchen with the weight of the rifle."

"Rifle?" Buller asked.

He had taken no notice of it and no more had I, but now out of nowhere the picture had come clear in my mind. When we had picked him up to carry him to his bed, there had been the guns on the kitchen floor and I was having this sudden certainty that it had been three guns there—the .45, Martha's shotgun, and a rifle.

"A rifle, I'm pretty sure," I said. "On the floor out there beside him. There are three guns lying there now, the two we brought in and the rifle."

"Are you going to be feeling guilty about it?" Buller asked.

I had to think about that for a moment or two.

"I could wish it hadn't been for me," I said.

"Why? Can you think of a way he would rather have gone?"

"Then he is going?"

"It isn't likely that he will ever be conscious again. In his last minutes of consciousness he was being what he wanted to be. I can rejoice for him in that. Think about it and you will, too."

It seemed to me that it was going to take a lot of thinking. I suppose I wasn't ready to work on it just then.

"I'd better get all those guns up off the kitchen floor," I said. "Loaded and lying around loose. They'll be better locked away."

"The boys," Buller said. "They'll be gone."

I'd forgotten them.

"It isn't possible that they haven't taken off," I said, "but wouldn't you have thought that we would have heard the motorcycles?"

"I don't think so," Buller said. "We've been too busy to notice. Also, even stupid as they are, they'd still have had sense enough to walk the bikes away from here until they were out of earshot."

He had to be right, but still I went out to look. Of course, they were gone. Coming back in through the kitchen, I picked up the guns. I unloaded the rifle and the shotgun. I left the unloaded shotgun in the kitchen. It was Martha Ainsley's, and it would have to be returned to her. The rifle I took to the gun case. It was locked, but the key was in the lock. I stowed the rifle, relocked the case, and pocketed the key. When I returned to Sam's room, I still had the loaded .45 with me.

"They did take off?" Buller said.

"How else?"

He looked pointedly at the .45.

"Then you won't be needing that."

"No. I won't."

Now he looked from the revolver to the table drawer.

"You want to put it back?" he asked.

"You knew?"

"That he was keeping it handy? No. I didn't know. I hope you won't mind my saying that you've been pretty transparent."

"It was always in his study, in the desk drawer. When I went for it tonight and it wasn't there, I had a hunch. He likely would have used it instead of going on the way he's been. My guess is that it was thinking of Millie that kept him from it."

"Certainly. You know him well enough for that."

"Obviously you know him that well, too," I said. "So now where, Doctor? You tell me where."

He shook his head.

"It has to be your decision," he said. "I can only tell you what I think I would do in your place."

"His gun," I said. "His life and his choice. Once I found it where it was, all that changed. Now I'll be making the choice for him, and it has me hung up. Put it back where he had it? Wouldn't that be going halfway toward killing him? Taking it back to the desk where he kept it in better times? Why do I feel that would be something like a betrayal?"

"Maybe because it *would* be something like," Buller said. "This I can tell you. Whatever it will be, it will be only in our minds, yours and mine. He'll never know and there's no possibility that he can come back out of this far enough to use it."

"You guarantee that?"

"There are never any guarantees, but my best opinion. He's on his way out and I'm keeping the promise I made to him. I'm going to set up an intravenous but only because Millie will be watching him and I want to make the watching less agonizing for her. But no heroic measure for another day or another hour or another anything when it can be nothing more than his being only technically alive."

"Then putting the revolver back will just be playing games," I said.

"It's for you and me, not for him," Buller said. "It's so we can tell ourselves that we never infringed on his dignity."

"I want to be able to tell myself that," I said.

I pulled the table drawer open and put the loaded revolver back where I'd found it. Buller watched me close the drawer.

"Now you tell me something," he said. "You've known her all her life. Should I be telling Millie?"

"About the gun in the drawer?"

"No need for that. I mean about where General Sam stands now."

"Yes," I said. "We don't infringe on her dignity either. She may want to be in here with him. Shouldn't it be her choice?"

"Of course," he said. "You couldn't be more right. It's only because it's Millie that I'm so mixed up about it. This wanting to protect her confuses everything."

"She's got Sam's blood in her. She doesn't need all that protecting."

"She doesn't," he said. "My trouble seems to be that I want her to be needing it."

I told myself that I shouldn't be a matchmaker and then I told myself that I had to speak for Sam.

"What you mean," I said, "is that you want her to be needing you. I've been wondering what's stopping you from seeing that she does."

"Money."

"The keeping-her-in-the-manner-to-which-she's-accustomed jazz? No problem there. She's well off and she'll be having Sam's money."

Buller scowled.

"A way of getting on in the world," he said. "It's not for me. A man has his role models. Creighton Douglas isn't mine."

"And you think Millie is some kind of Henry James heiress?"

"Not too different," Buller said. "It took only the first scent of what Douglas was after to make her drop him and fast."

"A fortune hunter readying himself for the leap from his wife's assets to Millie's. She'd have to be a fool not to have dropped him, and the girl's no fool."

"So what would make me different?"

"You being you and Douglas being Douglas. She never wanted him. He's just been for fun and that was only because you wouldn't play. She wants you, Doctor, and Sam wants you for her. How many signals do they have to give you?"

For just a moment he looked almost happy, but it was no more than the moment. He turned back to busy himself with his patient.

"It's a matter of the way I'd be seeing myself," he said.

There seemed to be nothing he had to do for Sam at that moment or nothing he could do for him. It was a good way for closing off the conversation.

"Okay if I send Millie in, or do you want me to tell her?"

"How it stands for General Sam?" he asked.

"That and how it stands for you and her," I said.

"Briefing her on the general is my job," Buller said. "Tell her I'd like her to come in."

"Meaning that the other is going to be my job?" I asked.

"If anything is to be said, that's also my job, but this isn't the time or the place."

I started out of the room, but in the doorway I turned for a last word.

"Do you want to wipe the lipstick off your face?" I asked. "Or can't you bear to part with it?"

Grinning, he rubbed at the lipstick smear.

"You might wash the blood off those scratches," he said. "Or do you like parading the walking-wounded look?"

I took off and sent Millie into the sickroom. There was a cupboard with mirror doors out in the hall. I caught a glimpse of my reflection in passing. Bloodied scratches, torn shirt, ripped pants, grass stains, and dirt smudges—I was a sorry sight. I went to my own room for a wash up and a change of clothes. Coming back out, I ran into Buller. He looked at the scratches. Washed, they were less spectacular than they had been, but they were still visible.

"How did you get those?" he asked.

"Blackberry bushes," I said.

"You're sure they didn't claw you some?"

"I'm sure."

"Okay," he said. "Then they'll be all right as they are."

"How's Millie?"

The question came from Martha Ainsley.

"Shaken and unhappy," Buller said. "It seemed to me that she wanted to be alone with General Sam for a while. She needs to cry and she won't let herself with people watching her."

"She'd be better doing it in your arms," Martha said. "If you had the sense you were born with, Jerry Buller, you'd be in there holding her tight."

He flushed.

"Everybody's pushing," he said.

The lady turned to me.

"Was there ever a man more in need of pushing?" she asked.

"Lay off, both of you," Buller said. "Has anybody called the troopers?"

I had a hunch that he didn't particularly want to know. He just wanted a change of subject. I looked to Martha Ainsley. She shook her head.

"Sam put those rascals right out of our minds," she said. "We forgot them completely. They'll be gone by now, of course."

"They're gone, but they shouldn't be too hard to find. I'll call the troopers."

I started for the phone, but Buller spoke up.

"It's your skin and your gas," he said. "I can't tell you that you should give it a by, but could you?"

"New skin grows," I said, "and the gas isn't all that important. I don't even know that they took any. They had a siphoning hose in the tank, but they could have just been playing games to bring me out of the house so that they could jump me. All that I could let pass, but a man's dead and he's dead of murder."

"That's it," Buller said. "It's a crazy time for them to be cutting up. Beebee's dead and it's got the town roused up. The kind of talk I've had from some of my most mild-mannered patients you wouldn't believe. This isn't lynching country around here, but . . ."

Martha broke in on him.

"Right now," she said, "it is lynching country. Oh, nobody's going to drag them from their beds and string them up out in the woods. That isn't our Down East style."

"No," Buller said. "We'll go through all the proper legal moves, but that won't keep any trial they get from being farcical."

I bypassed him to talk to Martha. I reminded her that she had been the one who had been all set to keep her shotgun on them while I called the State Troopers.

"You told me to make the call," I said. "Now you've changed your mind. Why?"

"For that very reason," she said. "I like to think that I know better, but in the heat of the moment with the shotgun in my hand, feeling like some kind of a Molly Pitcher or something equally ludicrous, I went lynch-minded. I've been thinking about that. If it could happen to Martha Ainsley, what can we expect of the idiots?"

"You're convinced that they didn't shoot Bean?" I asked.

"I've known them all their lives," she said.

I turned to Buller.

"And I know myself," he said. "If it hadn't been for General Sam, I would have been what they are. I would have been just like them. Hell, I was. I know what they are because I know what I was."

I came away from the telephone and left it untouched. Buller dropped his hand on my shoulder and squeezed. It meant that much to him. It was his way of thanking me. We left it at that, and he went back to the sickroom. I took Martha out to the Porsche and ran her up the road to her house. Along the road she started telling me about Dr. Jerry Buller, and back at her place she held me till she had finished her story.

"He wasn't exaggerating," she said. "He was a town boy and he was very much like this bunch of louts. It seems to me he was worse. He was the lout of louts. I suppose that was because he was brighter than any of the others."

CHAPTER 7

There aren't many people, even in Maine, who can match Martha Ainsley's boast. She was living in the house where she had been born and her father before her. In the course of her long life there had been periods when she had been away from it, but it had always been there in the background of her life. It had always been home base. So she knew the town and its history and its people as perhaps no one else could. She knew its constants and she had seen its changes.

She harked back to the years of her girlhood when there had been the year-rounders and the summer people. There were still the year-rounders and still the summer people. She was recalling the time when the summer people had been the owners of the "Maine cottages." There had been nothing modest about those "cottages" but their name. They had been the huge mansions set away in the isolation of the great estates. With their gatehouses and servants' wings and stables, their tennis courts and croquet greens and even golf courses, they had been almost completely self-contained.

"They were large families in the cottages," she said. "They didn't go into the town for their society. If they did any visiting, it was from estate to estate, and they had a constant coming and going of houseguests. They brought their staffs of servants with them from the cities. Occasionally, for a very big party, they might dip into the

town for extra help but even then there was virtually no
contact. The extra help dealt with a butler or a house-
keeper, just as the local tradesmen dealt with a house-
keeper or a coachman or a gardener. They were a world
apart and they had little effect on the year-rounders."

The young people of those days, she was saying, had
been all but unaware of their contemporaries in the
"Maine cottage" families. The year-rounders had their
own world of farming, lumbering, clamming, and fishing.
It was two worlds and next to no interplay between
them. All that, of course, had changed. The big families
were a thing of the past and the big houses were gone
and with them the great staffs of servants that could be
shifted about with the seasons. There were the couple of
remnants like Whatshisname down on Vinalhaven who
was never seen by his fellow islanders, not even in his ar-
rivals and departures since he came and went by his private jet and his private airstrip, and there was Whosis
over at Northeast Harbor who was similarly secluded
since his comings and goings were always by his yacht
which came into his private boat landing.

"The nearest thing to it that we have in the town now
might be the Douglas place. There's the private boat
landing and the big cabin cruiser, but imposing as that
may be, it's not an oceangoing, steam-driven yacht; and
Marian and Creighton go to the club for their golf and to
the club courts for their tennis. As you have reason to
know, they go to the post office for their mail. They do
their own dealing with the tradespeople and they are
here the year around."

There were still summer people, of course, but they
were no longer so much a world apart. They were more
visible and more accessible. The year-rounders knew
them. The year-rounders were all too aware of summer-

people affluence, familiar with summer-people luxuries and pleasures.

"The new Mercedes parks on Main Street alongside the wheezing jalopy," she said. "The contrasts and comparisons are always there and they are abrasive. But that is only part of the change. The big estates are gone and they have been replaced by beautiful, small waterfront parcels with beautiful, small houses. With this parceling out, land values have increased enormously and taxes on waterfront property have rocketed. It's far more expensive than it used to be for people like Sam and me, but we can carry it. Most of the year-rounders have been feeling the pinch. What was their farmland can no longer be farmed for even a small profit. Their land has become too valuable for farming and they cannot afford to hold it. They are being squeezed out, and their young people have lost the roots that young people here used to have in the land and the water."

Her point was clear. What the cottage kids had, however rich and splendid it may have been, had never seemed accessible. It had also been virtually invisible to the kids of the town. What this later breed of summer people had and what their kids enjoyed seemed as though it should have been accessible even though, of course, it was not.

"So now we have these miserable lads," she said. "They work only when they must and only as much as they must. They live cheaply but only because they live like pigs. They work only to pay for their motorcycles and to keep them going. There's that and there's beer and they grow constantly more loutish. But that's the extent of it. They are loutish. They aren't evil."

"And Jerry Buller, M.D.?" I asked.

"Yes. When he was their age and younger, things were

much as they are now for the kids except that there weren't the motorcycles. I mean that, although there were motorcycles, boys had not yet taken them up, much less made a cult of them. So it was quieter then without the dreadful din of those misbegotten things. Otherwise, though, it was worse. Car theft was a constant thing. Cars wouldn't be permanently lost. They would take them to go joyriding and carousing and, when they ran out of gas, they would abandon them by the roadside. Jerry Buller went joyriding in Sam's Cadillac and Sam caught him."

She knew the whole story and, knowing Sam as I did, I could well understand that it had gone just as Sam would have had it go. He had offered the kid a choice. Sam could turn him over to the police and charge him with car theft or the thing could be kept just between the two of them. Young Buller chose to keep it between the two of them.

"Sam," she said, "put it on a dollar-and-cents basis."

He told the boy what the rental charges by the hour would be on a Cadillac such as Sam's. He figured up the sum of what the lad owed him on that basis and he told young Jerry that he would have to work the debt off.

The kid had accepted the deal and Sam had put him to work. He worked him hard and he stood over him, keeping him at it. By the time the kid had worked himself into the clear, he had become Sam's boy.

"He went on working for Sam. He caddied for him. He did the heavy work in the garden. They came to be friends and, since Jerry was bright and Sam was showing him the way, the rest followed. A scholarship and working his way through college. Then it was medical school on a loan from Sam and now we have a far better doctor than you'd expect to find in a town this size; Jerry Buller is a fine doctor and a good man. He's good enough for Millie and that has to be very good indeed."

"And that explains the way he feels and the way you feel," I said. "But who's to take on the lot of them the way Sam took on the one?"

She sighed.

"They're not every one of them a Jerry Buller," she said, "but one would like to think they aren't beyond salvaging. You caught them red-handed and at a time when, even in their stupidity, they will have to realize that prejudice was running hot against them. I don't think jail will make them come to their senses. A realization that they have been the recipients of an act of civilized generosity, of sympathetic forbearance mightn't do it either, but don't you think it's more likely to?"

"I don't know," I said. "They're more likely to think I'm just a sap who can be pushed around."

"And that would be a dreadful injury to your vanity?"

"It's not my chosen image, but, if that's the way they will think, how good will it be for bringing them to their senses?"

"I was there," she said, "and Jerry Buller was there. They know that we aren't saps who can be pushed around."

"There are those who would call you a pair of bleeding hearts," I said.

"There are those," she said.

Her tone said they were not worth the consideration of Martha Ainsley.

"Okay," I said. "They were siphoning gas out of the Porsche. They didn't take all of it since Baby had enough left in her tank to let me run you back here. Still, with gas prices what they are today plus the cost of a wrecked shirt and a ripped pair of slacks, I can add the thing up.

Would you think I should go find them and offer them Sam's choice?"

It wasn't a serious suggestion, but she took it as though it might be.

"You could work it out with Jerry Buller. You could tell them that he's paying you for your losses and they'll have to work it off on jobs he'll give them. You'll be going away, but Jerry will be here and he won't let them off easy."

I dismissed the idea. With the debt divided five ways, it would come down to something that would look more like pettiness than generosity. With evident regret she agreed.

I ran Baby back to Sam's driveway. Buller's car was gone. Sam seemed to be much as he had been when I'd last seen him, but now with a blear-eyed Dexter in attendance. Dexter said there had been no change, and Buller had gone to the hospital to look in on patients he had there. He would be back.

I asked about Millie. Dexter said that on Buller's assurance that there would be no change in the immediate future and on Dexter's promise that he would call her if there was anything, she had been persuaded to go to her room to catch some sleep.

"She went when the doctor left," Dexter said. "She knew he wouldn't be going if anything quick was going to happen."

I had the thought that it could be smart for Erridge to follow her example. I should have been sleeping while I could just so that I might be awake if it came a time when I might be needed. When I came out of the sickroom, however, Mathilda was waiting in the hall. She jumped all over me. It was obvious that she had other ideas. It was hours now since anyone had given her any notice, and she had been a good dog. Now she wanted a run. Certainly she had earned one.

I did need sleep but I had also been a long time sitting around indoors. A good lungful of that fresh sea air the dawn breezes were bringing ashore and a brief leg stretch could have been a great preliminary to sleep. Pretending that I was indulging Mathilda, I thus far indulged myself. We went out for what was to have been a brief morning run. We went down through the garden and over the stretch of lawn. We were headed down to the beach. We knew that beach, Mathilda and I. It was the best place for running. At the edge of the lawn, before we started down the rock path, I was stopped for a moment by a peculiar sight.

The water was dead calm. In the early light it looked like a stretch of silver satin shot here and there with color reflected off some puffs of cloud that, at the farthest reach of the sunrise glow, were turning pink.

It was pretty, but for sunrise stuff it was usual enough. There was nothing peculiar about it, and there was nothing peculiar about the half dozen small boats dotted here and there out on the bay. Those would be the lobstermen pulling in their traps to bring in the catch. The lobstermen were out there every day at first light. They were a familiar sight. What was peculiar was what I could see of the activity of some of them. Those were busily hauling stuff into their boats but what those were hauling was not coming up out of the deeps down where the lobsters live. It was something else. It was floating on the surface.

Promising myself that I would ask about it, I started to go on down to the beach. Mathilda had gone off to the shrubbery at the edge of the lawn. She was lunging and barking. I don't know that she has ever been serious about catching a rabbit, but from time to time she seems to get the idea that it might suit her image as a serious dog of affairs to take on the stance of a dog who hunts rabbits. I whistled and started down the path. She would be coming along after me in her own good time and, if she didn't, she was all right where she was. So were the rabbits.

As soon as I hit the flat, I saw it. It was snagged on a rock at the water's edge, half washed up on the beach but with the legs trailing in the water. The rock on which it was snagged had it firmly anchored. The face was nothing recognizable. It didn't even look much like a face. That happens when a body comes up out of the sea unless it has been brought up quickly after death. In the Aran Islands, when a fisherman drowns and his body washes up, he is identified by his sweater. Each wife knows the pattern of her own knitting.

So now I knew this dead man by his clothes. It was Creighton Douglas. He was dressed just as he had been when I had last seen him. One item, however, had been added. There was a length of rope tightly secured around his waist and from it hung a canvas sack. The sack lay limp, more than half empty. I felt of it. What was in the sack was something hard, like a small rock, but it wasn't a rock. Under the pressure of my fingers I felt the surface of it crumble away into small granules and then those quickly dissolved. There was black lettering on the sack. I spread the canvas enough so that I could read it. It read: ROCK SALT—50 LB. BLOCK.

I didn't stand around down there thinking about it. I did my thinking on the run, heading back to the house and the telephone. Obviously now all bets were off. On this I had no choice but to call the State Troopers. It was clear enough. Creighton Douglas hadn't just walked out on his watch over Beebee Bean's body. He had been killed. His body had been thrown into the water weighted down with a fifty-pound block of rock salt. Feet encased in cement or a cement block fastened to his waist would have been better for a long-term effect, but a killer may have to make do with what is available.

That made sense but it left me asking myself what could have made a fifty-pound block of rock salt available down on the beach that previous night. I knew about blocks of the stuff put out as a lick for animals, but I couldn't imagine anyone setting one out on the beach.

Mathilda was still on the lawn putting on her hunting-dog act. I hauled her away from it. I didn't want to leave her out there long enough for her to lose interest in it. Without an audience she would lose interest. She might go on down to the beach to play games with the body.

The telephone operator put me through to the Town Hall. The troopers who were working on the Bean killing had set themselves up a headquarters there. Trooper Steve Boudreau came on. I gave him a quick rundown on the body.

"Not an accidental drowning," I said. "A fifty-pound block of rock salt in a canvas sack was tied to the body to sink it. In twenty-four hours most of the salt dissolved. We can figure the body surfaced during the night."

Boudreau jumped on it.

"Hey," he said. "Just the body? Did you see anything else? Is there anything floating around on the bay?"

"Some stuff," I said. "The lobstermen are out there. I saw four of them hauling it in."

Boudreau was impatient with me.

"I don't mean lobster pots," he said. "Stuff like the body, held down till the salt dissolved enough for the thing to bob up on the surface."

"I don't know about anything submerged that's now

bobbing up," I said, "but it could be. What I saw was stuff floating on the surface. It wasn't lobster pots."

"Right," Boudreau said. He sounded breathless. He was hurried and excited. "I'll get this to the Coast Guard. I'll be right over. Watch the lobstermen till I get there. Get a count on how many of them are out there."

With that he hung up. I went into Sam's room for his binoculars. Dexter was at the window. He was looking out at the bay and, of course, combing his hair. I planted myself beside him and focused the glasses. They were good glasses. They brought everything in close and clear. The lobster boats were still out there, but now they were back to normal. I could see the guys as they hauled up their lobster traps. I could even see them taking the lobsters out and tossing the undersized ones back into the bay. I could see them rebait the traps and drop them overside. There was no sign of the things I had seen some of them haul in earlier, no sign of anything afloat on the bay, nothing but the lobster boats.

Those I could see so well that I could read the names and numbers painted on them. I started snapping orders at Dexter.

"Get a pad and pencil," I said. "Write these down as I give them to you."

It seemed to me that he should have jumped to it. Certainly I was being peremptory enough, but this was Dexter. Dexters are Dexters. You don't catch them doing anything that isn't strictly part of their job, not without a good explanation and some considerable amount of persuasion.

"There's been another killing," I said. "Dead man washed up on the beach. The troopers want a count of the lobstermen. We can do better than that for them."

"Killing?" Dexter asked. "Why not an accidental drowning?"

I couldn't tell whether he wanted to know or he was just making talk until he would have finished combing his hair, not that he ever seemed to finish with that.

"With a weight attached to sink the body? Leave your goddamn hair alone. It's pretty enough for Hollywood."

"Suicide," Dexter said. "A man's a good swimmer. No way he can drown himself without he fixes it so he'll be dragged down."

"Okay. Okay. But the troopers want a count on the lobstermen. Let's get it for them."

Dexter stowed the comb and came up with a pad and pencil. I started reading off the boat names and numbers. I had to do a lot of repeating because Dexter wouldn't shut up to listen and write. He came up with another argument.

"The body didn't stay down," he said. "If it was a killing, he'd have been weighted so that he'd stay down, wouldn't he? A suicide, he wants to be held down long enough so he drowns, not forever so he'll never be found."

"Shut up and write what I'm giving you," I said.

It wasn't that his argument was convincing me, but that there seemed to be just enough sense in it to make me feel that it called for consideration. I wanted some time for thinking about it.

The lobster boats were still out there when Boudreau came roaring into the driveway. The boats kept moving about as the lobstermen shifted from one of their traps to the next, but none of them was taking off. They were all still out there, hauling in their catch.

I gave Boudreau the list Dexter had written down from

my dictation and I went back down to the beach with the trooper. Mathilda wanted to come along, but even though she gave me her best you're-playing-me-dirty-pal stance, I made her stay in the house. Boudreau was carrying a bullhorn.

"This is beginning to shape out," he said, as we trotted through the garden and across the lawn. "It's drug smuggling. Waterproof bales weighted down with blocks of salt. They're surprised by any kind of law, Coast Guard or whatever, they just heave the cargo over the side and they're clean. They know how long it will take for the salt to dissolve. They're waiting when the stuff comes afloat and they haul it in."

"The lobstermen?" I asked.

"They're the ones hauling it in, aren't they?"

"Yes," I said, "but not during the night, not when it was still dark. Why would they wait till daylight when everybody and his brother could see them do it?"

"First light when they could see what they were doing," Boudreau said. "First light when they would have a legitimate reason for being out on the water. It's the time of day when they are always out to tend to their lobster pots. First light when everybody and his brother along this stretch of the shore will be asleep. That's the way it goes. Guys think they have everything figured so it'll be perfectly safe, but someone turns up in the wrong place at the wrong time. He oughtn't be there, but it happens he is. There's no way they can figure that. Why would they ever think you would be out and about to watch the sunrise? Anyhow, for watching the sunrise you'd be looking the other way. It rises in the east."

"I don't know," I said.

"If it wasn't for this kind of thing," Boudreau said, "someone like you just happening to turn up in the wrong place at the wrong time, smart crooks would hardly ever get caught."

This wasn't nonsense the man was talking. I had to concede that much; but, nevertheless, I couldn't make the thing jell into what would look like any reasonable pattern. We had come down onto the beach and with the aid of his bullhorn Trooper Boudreau was roaring his orders out to the lobster boats. He told them to stay where they were. He told them that the Coast Guard was coming around to bring them in. He told them that they had no place to run.

"You're under observation," he shouted. "So don't throw anything overboard. We know who you are and we're watching you."

He had begun by identifying himself. I could see them out on the bay. Nobody was trying to make a run for it. Nobody was doing anything. It was obvious that they had heard. They were just out there, sitting frozen in their boats.

I was thinking about the arguments he had thrown at me. He was right about one thing. It was only through the odd and unforeseeable succession of accidents that I had happened to see them. If it hadn't been for the kids' raiding Baby's gas tank, Sam wouldn't have had his stroke or, if it had been coming in any case, he would have had it in his sleep and I would have slept the night away without knowing. If it hadn't been for all that time that had gone by while Martha Ainsley was telling me the Jerry Buller story and filling me in on history and social change, I would have taken Mathilda for her run earlier when it would still have been dark. If it hadn't been for Mathilda, I wouldn't have postponed hitting the sack even for as long as it had taken for the stroll down to the beach. The lobstermen couldn't have foreseen any part of that. Nobody could have conceived the whole of it.

Conceding that much, however, I came up against the things I just couldn't accept. Those were lobstermen out there. I can't say I knew all of them, but I knew two or three. No man possessed of any sort of palate could be in those parts for any length of time without knowing at least one lobsterman. Along that coast you'd have to be the most insensate clod to live by pizza alone.

More than that, I knew the breed. Salty, weather-beaten types who live by lobstering don't run in packs. They are loners. It's a man and his boat, a man and the weather, a man and the tides and the winds. I wasn't going to take my oath that there wasn't any one of them who mightn't go for a sideline of drug smuggling, but I was prepared to take my oath that it would have to be a one-man operation. Cooperation in a criminal enterprise couldn't ever have been their style.

There was that, but there was also the way this thing had begun. Lobstermen down on the beach that night when Beebee Bean was killed? Lobstermen giggling and hooting while they were engaged in an operation that demanded silence and secrecy? They couldn't have been that stupid and beyond everything they weren't gigglers. That part of it had been more in the style of the motorcycle kids, though even there I was having difficulty conceiving of the kids' being that stupid.

All the same, they did seem to be the more likely, but there again the next thought stopped me cold. I could talk myself into believing that they might be right for that beginning, but now they seemed impossibly wrong for the sequel. What had they been doing messing around with my Porsche just at the time when they should have been out on the bay retrieving their cargo?

These were local kids. They had lived on this coast all their lives. It couldn't be that they wouldn't know where the lobster traps were and it couldn't be that they wouldn't know that at first light the lobstermen would be out doing the rounds of their traps.

That seemed to clinch it. My thinking swung back to the lobstermen, but that was a quickly aborted swing. It came up against the solid obstacle of Creighton Douglas' body and the salt block used for sinking it. Day after day these men went out to haul up their traps, remove the catch, replace the bait and sink the traps. If there was anyone who would know all there was to know about how to sink something and make it stay down, it would be a lobsterman. For that matter, I couldn't see how anyone who had spent the whole of his life along these waters could not have known. Beyond that, where would you go to find someone who doesn't know that salt is soluble in water?

Actually there was no need for making any guesses about that. The choice of the block of salt as the sinker weight could have been made with only one purpose in mind—to make the sinking not only temporary but also of reasonably calculable duration. Whoever it had been who had sunk the parcels I'd seen the lobstermen haul in would necessarily have known that everything would come bobbing up at about the same time, the body along with the rest of it.

It was no good saying that the salt had been used for the body because it was ready to hand, and in an emergency a man will make do with what is available. That's a rock-strewn coast, and this was New England. Where in that part of the continent are you going to find even a small stretch of country where you could lack for a handy hunk of rock?

Even while I was doing all this thinking, Trooper Boudreau was examining the body.

"Autopsy will maybe tell us for sure," he said, "but it don't look like he drowned. Somebody picked up a rock and knocked his skull in before putting the body in the water. If he wasn't already dead when he went under, he was at least dying."

He suggested that we look along the beach for a rock. He wanted one with blood and bits of hair and scalp stuck to it. I spent a few minutes turning over rocks and finding nothing he could want. He called me off it.

"We'll comb the beach for it," he said, having second thoughts. "So skip it for now. There probably won't be anything anyhow. It would have been too easy for the guy to heave the rock into the water when he was finished with it, just as easy as dropping it on the beach and that way it would be washed clean by now."

"Even on the beach," I said. "It was ebb tide when I left Douglas here. The water has come up over the beach again and again since then."

Boudreau whacked me on the back.

"That's thinking," he said. "We can forget the rock."

I took issue with that.

"Can we?" I asked.

"Sure we can. It could be any of these rocks. Every tide has given them a wash."

"That's not what I'm thinking," I said. "You pick up a rock and you knock a man's head in. You kill him. So now you have two things you want to dispose of—the body and the murder weapon. Why do you use a block of salt to sink the body? You know that he'll come bobbing up as soon as enough of the salt has dissolved. You know that because it's what you have the salt there for. Why don't you dump the salt out of the sack and replace it with the rock? It's a much better sinker and it's also the murder weapon you want out of the way."

"Killing two birds with one stone," Boudreau said. "If all killers were smart or even if a possibly smart one didn't go stupid in the excitement and stress of killing, there wouldn't be many of them caught."

It was a way of looking at it, but it left all the questions unanswered. They were whizzing around in my head, those questions, and I was getting nowhere with them. Just for a respite, I switched to a different one. Unexpectedly, that one did have some sort of an answer.

"The tide washed the body ashore," I said, "but only the body. The stuff they were hauling in out there on the bay, that stayed put."

"Right," Boudreau said. "It's the way they do it. The block of salt is fastened tight to the package, but there is also a second weight. It's stone or concrete, anyhow something that won't dissolve. That weight is fastened to the package by a long line. Done that way, the package bobs up where it was dropped and it holds there on the surface till you cut the line and pull it aboard."

So there it was—some sort of an answer but only some sort because, if anything, it put a sharper point on the earlier question. If the equipment was as Boudreau described it, made up of two weights, a soluble one and a second that would stay down, why would the body have been fastened to the soluble weight and not to the other one? The salt and the long line could have been eliminated. With the body fastened tight to the other weight, it would have remained submerged.

I asked the question and Boudreau shrugged it off.

"He didn't want it anchored. He wanted it to drift

when it came up. He overlooked the possibility that it would drift ashore. He was figuring the tide would carry it out to sea."

"It didn't drift ashore. The tide washed it ashore."

"Same difference, mister."

"The tides and the currents," I said. "The lobstermen know them. They have to know them."

"Sure. And murderers panic and in their panic they forget everything they ever knew."

It was a puzzle and I could think of no better solution to it, but, nevertheless, I couldn't quite buy it. "Everything they ever knew" struck me as much too sweeping. In panic a man might forget almost anything, but there are things that are bred in the bone, like a waterman's knowledge of wind and tide. Those, I was thinking, couldn't be forgotten.

I kept my reservations to myself. For the time being, at least, I hadn't much choice. It was just then that the Coast Guard boat came whamming in and Boudreau was having no ears for me. There was a bullhorn exchange between ship and shore. Then it was a Coast Guard operation that was something to watch. The whole thing couldn't have been more efficient or more orderly. So far as I could see from the shore, it looked easy. The lobstermen, it appeared, were being docile and cooperative. They converged on the Coast Guard boat and climbed aboard. The Coast Guard people took over on the lobster boats, lashing them together and tethering them to the Coast Guarder's stern.

Trooper Boudreau watched only long enough to satisfy himself that it was a clean sweep. Then he turned away.

"I'm going up to the phone," he said. "Can I ask you to hang on here with the body until I can get my guys in to take over from you?"

I knew what he was thinking. This wasn't the first time someone had been left on this beach to stand by a body till the police would come. He was thinking that I couldn't but have that in mind. It could have been that I would be having misgivings about volunteering for such duty.

"I'll be here," I said. "I'll be here and watching my back."

That won me one of his approving whacks on the shoulder.

"It won't be like the other night when we had to come all the way from our barracks," he said. "I've got my boys set up in the Town Hall. It'll only be a couple of minutes."

"My breakfast can wait that long," I said.

He told me that I would be wanted over at the Town Hall. He planned to confront the lobstermen with me and with my account of what I had seen.

"Don't hurry your breakfast for it," he said. "They won't be going anywhere and it'll be all to the good if they have to sit and sweat for a while."

"Hey, Boudreau," I said. "The presumption of innocence? Where did it go?"

"That's for the courts," he said. "It's for the judge and the jury. It's not for a cop."

He was as good as his word. He had his men down on the beach in record time. Back at the house the air was full of breakfast smells—fresh coffee, sizzling bacon, johnnycake. Those smells had never been more mouthwatering, but I was resolute. Swallowing the flood, I skirted the breakfast table. First I was going to check in on Sam. He seemed much as he had been except that now it wasn't Dexter with him. It was Jerry Buller.

"You heard about Douglas?" I asked.

"The idiot told me. That Dexter!"

"Yes. That Dexter! You spelling him while he sleeps or is he off giving himself a new hairdo?"

"Combing his hair?" Buller said. "For that he doesn't go off. Anytime and anywhere. No. I sent him over to the hospital to get a lot of stuff we need for General Sam. The idiot has let practically everything run out. I swear, if you had been around to take over in here, I would have gone with him just so I could kick his ass all the way over and all the way back. To let himself get so short on everything, it's inconceivable."

"Stuff you need for Sam?" I asked. "Wasn't it a promise? When it came to this, no heroic measures for keeping him going on this way?"

"Right," Buller said, "but no bedsores either."

The way he handed me the word, it was like a slap.

"Sorry," I said.

"Forget it. Have you told the troopers about the kids?"

"No, I haven't. I decided I wouldn't. Now with this new killing, I'm thinking maybe I should."

"Why?"

"For them," I said. "In a remote way it might serve to clear them."

Buller had trouble understanding that. There was every reason why he should have been finding it difficult.

"The troopers tagging them for the Douglas killing?" he asked.

Even though he'd had the word from Dexter and Dexter had been calling it a suicide, Buller said "killing."

"Not so far," I said. "Right now they're zeroed in on the lobstermen who work out from here. I can't believe they'll find any way to make that stick. Then the kids will be next in line."

All the time we were talking, I was swallowing. He no-

ticed it and he read the symptom. How could a good doctor ever have missed on that? He grinned on me.

"When a man salivates at the rate you're going," he
said, "I prescribe immediate breakfast. You go get it. I'll
join you as soon as that gold-bricking bastard gets back.
He's good at his job, none better, but you give him any
time away from his patient and you can be sure he'll
stretch it."

"He been gone long?"

"If I had gone myself, I'd have been back before this,
but I wouldn't have stopped for a lot of stupid chatter.
You've been around long enough to know. There's nothing about the guy that's as busy as his tongue."

"Unless it's his comb," I said.

"You can call it a dead heat," Buller said. "Go get your
breakfast. You'll tell me over the coffee how you think
you can help the kids."

He wasn't long. I wasn't more than past the orange
juice when he joined me. Over the bacon and eggs and
johnnycake I gave him the complete fill-in, everything I'd
seen, everything I'd heard from Trooper Boudreau, everything that I had been thinking. He heard me out, and
at every point he was seeing it my way.

"If it was the kids," I said, "then why, just at the very
time when they should have been out on the water to salvage the stuff that was due to surface during the night,
would they have been up here to mess with my gas tank?
All right, they are young dopes and all that. They haven't
got good sense, but still first things first. Getting even
with me, that could have waited."

"It wasn't the kids," Buller said. "That's for sure. You
know, Dexter is no brain, but on this he might just have
hit it right. He thinks Douglas was a suicide."

"Doctor," I said, "you've been working too hard. The

man picks up a rock and knocks his own head in. Then, oozing brain all the time, he fastens that fifty-pound block of salt to his waist and hauls himself far enough out so that it'll be deep enough to submerge him."

Buller chuckled.

"It didn't have to be that way," he said. "He could have fastened the block of salt to himself before he knocked himself on the head. Not that it wouldn't have been impossible even that way. Your trooper thinks he sees a head wound and he interprets it in the way that most readily will come to a policeman's mind. Bodies that come up out of the water can be deceptive. The damage to the head could be *postmortem*. Your man Boudreau is jumping to conclusions that can be established only by an autopsy, if they can be established at all."

"Okay," I said. "Then we accept suicide as one possibility. Any ideas on why he would?"

"He'd put himself in a lousy spot. It looks like he burned his bridges with his wife in his mistaken certainty that he was going to be able to jump to Millie. He made the error of not making sure of Millie first. So that night she had only just finished telling him that there wasn't a hope. She wasn't even going to let him work on it. She wasn't going to be seeing him anymore. So there he was. He couldn't go forward and he couldn't go back. He was on the brink of being stuck with having to work for a living. That wasn't for Crate Douglas. He would rather have died."

"I don't read him that way," I said. "I'd say he was a guy who would tell himself that there would always be another woman."

"Another woman with the means it takes to keep him in the manner to which he was accustomed?"

"Does Millie know about him?"

"That he's dead? No. She's still asleep. I promised her she'd be wakened if there was any change in General Sam. She doesn't need to be wakened to be told about Douglas."

CHAPTER 8

What with all this talk, Buller and I were long at the breakfast table. I looked at my watch. It was more than time for me to have been over to the Town Hall. Trooper Boudreau's catch of lobstermen had sweated out far more waiting time than he could possibly have planned for them.

I headed over there only to be told I wasn't needed. The lobstermen were no longer in custody. They had been turned loose. I found only Trooper Steve Boudreau and Coast Guardsman Phil England closeted together. The two of them were plunged in the deepest gloom. At first sight I had the impression that it was a despondency that was alleviated by nothing but outbursts of rage.

They brightened some, but that was only while they were showing me the confiscated goods. It was marijuana, four bales of the weed. Phil England, out of his Coast Guard expertise in the matter, was putting its market worth at six figures and he was talking a fat six. So much, so good. They had the grass, but it was all they had. The lobstermen had been turned loose.

"They had nothing to do with it," Boudreau said. "They were nowhere near the beach when Bean was shot and everything says Douglas was murdered that same night. It was also that night the stuff was smuggled in. So they had nothing to do with that either."

"They just found it afloat when they went out to their

lobster pots this morning," England said. "They found it and hauled it in. Maybe they were going to hand it over to us and maybe they were going to try to go into the business. They say they were going to hand it over to us. I can have my doubts about that; but, since they never had the time to do anything with it one way or the other, we'll never know."

"And you can't charge men with what they might have done if they'd had the time," I said.

"Yeah," Boudreau said. "We had to turn them loose and now we've got nobody."

This was a different Boudreau from the man I'd talked to a couple of hours before. I couldn't believe that he had turned the lobstermen loose on nothing more than their simple protestations of innocence.

"What changed your mind about them?" I asked.

"Alibis," England said.

"They've got iron-bound, copper-plated, watertight alibis, every last one of them," Boudreau said.

The way he sounded, you could have thought that innocence was the worst of all possible crimes.

"So it's those motorcycle kids," England said.

"And we've lost them, too," Boudreau said. "They've taken off, disappeared, all five of them, every last one of the little bastards. Nobody thought they'd have any place to go."

I wanted to remind him about how wrong he had been about the lobstermen. I was casting about for a more tactful way of putting it. While I was working that one out, I temporized.

"The lobstermen?" I asked. "What kind of alibis?"

"The best kind," England said.

Boudreau elaborated. The night of the Bean murder there had been an early-morning fire—a house on the other side of the neck. Those lobstermen all belong to the firehouse volunteers. When Bean was killed, they were all miles away, fighting the fire. That also went for when the waterproof bales of marijuana were dumped and for the time when Douglas was killed.

"They couldn't have better alibis," England said. "They're covered every which way and for every possible minute of the time."

"By their firehouse buddies?" I asked.

"Them and the people whose house burned and the people's neighbors who came out of their houses to watch and the neighbor women who gave them coffee and doughnuts and brownies after they had the fire out."

"Yeah," Boudreau said, "and meanwhile we've let them others slip away from us."

"We were wrong about the lobstermen," I said.

I was hoping the person switch on the pronoun would take care of any problems of tact. Trooper Boudreau was a stricken man. I wasn't out to inflict any additional wounds.

"I was wrong about them," Boudreau said. He was not a man to grab at even the small measure of shelter I'd offered him. "But now this is different. If it wasn't the kids, why would they have pulled their disappearance act?"

"How does it go?" England said. "Only the guilty flee where no man pursueth."

"Close enough," I said. "The question is guilty of what? I think I know."

"I do know," Boudreau said. "You maybe think you know, but I don't think. I know."

"So now maybe you can try thinking," I said, throwing tact to the winds. "I have something I can tell you."

"Like what?"

"Like they're running away from me."

"Because yesterday morning they let the air out of your tires?"

"Because just at the time when the marijuana smugglers should have been out on the water waiting for the bales to come floating up, they were, the whole gang of them, in General Dalton's driveway beating up on me."

I gave them the full rundown on that action. Boudreau wasn't liking any of it.

"Assault," he said, "and you didn't report it. It's people like you makes kids think they can get away with anything."

"Assault," I said. "I'm the one who started it. Yesterday morning in the post office I slapped one of them around. Did he report it?"

Boudreau indicated that he expected that of kids. They would take the law into their own hands. He had expected better of me.

"Not when it's a fight I know I started."

Maybe I was drawing a fine point, but it was there to be drawn. It hadn't been me the young lout had kicked. It had been Mathilda.

"So now they're scared of you?" Boudreau asked. "Now when they weren't before?"

I spelled it out for him. So far as the kids could have known, I had been about to call the troopers. They had no way of knowing that I had changed my mind and that I had no intention of bringing charges against them.

"They're thinking they had a narrow squeak," I said, "and that just taking off and staying out of sight for a while they'll be okay. Everybody knows that General Dalton is dying and that I'm up here only to be with him through his last hours, days, what have you. They're thinking that they have to lie low just until the general is gone. I'll be pulling out, and that will be that. I won't be around to press any charges against them."

Boudreau wasn't convinced, but it wasn't that he was skeptical about the picture I was drawing for him. It was simply that he didn't want to be convinced. He all but said as much.

"It's got to be them," he said. "There isn't anyone else."

Of the two of them, Coast Guardsman England was the less unhappy.

"We've got the marijuana at least," he said. "That's a lot. They weren't successful in bringing it in. We're not always that lucky."

"Lucky!" Boudreau was outraged. "We've got two murders still on our hands. You call that lucky?"

I was tempted to relay to him the medical opinion I'd had from Jerry Buller on the subject of dead bodies that come up out of the water. I didn't do it because I could see no profit in it. Even on that remote possibility that Creighton Douglas' death had been a suicide, there was not the slightest chance of doubt about the death of Officer Burton Bean. Even at best, Trooper Boudreau had one murder on his hands.

I tried to tell myself that I should walk away from it. It was Steve Boudreau's problem. It wasn't mine. I wasn't a cop. I hadn't come up to Maine to do my bit for law and order. I was there to be with Sam, and it was time I took myself back to the house, leaving it to the law to take care of the law. All this that I was trying to tell myself made the best of sense, but Martha Ainsley and Jerry Buller between them had planted a thought in my mind.

I hadn't tried to cultivate it, but quite on its own it had been growing and it was coming to the place where it

threatened to take over. I couldn't get it out of my head
that in a curious way I, Matthew Erridge, had come to be
responsible for the fix these young devils were in.

You can ask in what way responsible. I was asking that
myself. I couldn't make it that I was carrying the full re-
sponsibility. Their stupidity, their idleness, and their dev-
iltry were no fault of mine. On the other hand, they
were putting themselves in jeopardy of an accusation of
murder. That is no small thing at any time and in any
place, but then and there, with the lynch spirit running
high, it was more than ever dangerous. I was convinced
that it was only because of me that they had skipped out
and gone into hiding, but in the mind of Trooper Steve
Boudreau their flight was all that had been needed to
convict them of murder. Trooper Boudreau's mind was a
police officer's mind. To some extent at least it was a
mind trained in such matters. How was this going to be
perceived in the minds of the town's vindictive inno-
cents?

It was only a step or two to Jerry Buller's office, only
across the street and around the corner into the Common.
I took that couple of steps and brought my troubled mind
to the doctor. I didn't have to go into any details on my
thinking. His was running too closely on the same lines.
He had nothing comforting he could offer me. He
couldn't find any comfort for himself.

"I'm pretty sure I know where those idiots have gone
to hide," he said. "I've been thinking I ought to go after
them. They need somebody who'll talk some sense to
them, but it would be two to three hours at least and I
have General Sam and other patients, too. I can't just
take off and be out of touch for half a day or more."

"Could I go?" I asked.

"It'll take finding, but I could tell you. Do you think

they'll listen to you? I could make them listen to me. I've helped them other times when they've been in trouble. It was never anything big like this, but it looked big to them."

"I can try," I said.

"Would you? How about this afternoon?"

"What about right now?"

"Right now," he said, "there's something else. I'm going to ask a favor of you."

"Sure. Anything I can do."

"Go back to the house. I'm stuck here and in the hospital for the rest of the morning. I don't anticipate any immediate change in General Sam's condition. If there is anything, Dexter will call me and I can be over there in a minute, but it's Millie. I don't like her being without anyone, and I've made Martha Ainsley go to bed. Last night didn't do her any good. So till afternoon there's nobody. I'll be there in the afternoon."

"Millie was all right last night," I said. "She's Sam's granddaughter. She's got the stuff."

"She's got too much of the stuff," he said. "She's being the good soldier and all that crap. There's questionable benefit in the good-soldier business. Good soldiers take the worst emotional beating."

"Right," I said. "I'll go and hold her hand till you can take over. I don't have to tell you it isn't bad duty."

"I wish I had the right to tell you not to enjoy it too much."

"The right's there, Jerry. Grab for it."

He didn't pick that up.

"You'll be taking a load off my mind," he said.

"My pleasure. But about the kids, what makes you think you know where to find them?"

"There was a time when I was running with their uncles," Buller said. "It's where we used to go when we were in trouble. In their time it was where our uncles went and maybe our fathers, too, but our fathers reached for the strap and pretended that they'd never been young and they'd never been in trouble. It was a good place back then and with every year that passes it gets to be a better place. Those things get passed on down."

"Are you the only man in town who remembers being young?"

"The guys I ran with? Some of them are long gone from around here. The others, if they haven't worked at forgetting, they think the kids are up for murder. They won't give them away, but they won't turn a hand to help them either."

"You know your town," I said.

"I know my people."

I went back to the house, and it was none too soon. Millie wasn't alone. She had Marian Douglas with her. Don't get the idea that the woman was making even a feeble stab at acting the grieving widow. She wasn't even putting on any pretense of being in shock. The dame was all ice and acid. Even before I'd hauled out of Baby I could hear her from the driveway.

"I want to know what happened here the night my husband died," she was screaming. "I demand to know, and you are going to tell me."

"I've already told you," Millie was saying when I walked in on them.

My first thought was that it was well that Sam's condition prevented his hearing any of this. A second thought was that it was too bad that it should have come when he was in no shape for taking a hand and dealing with the bitch. I opened my mouth with the passing idea that it might devolve on me to deal for him, but I looked at

Millie and I shut it without saying a word. This was Millie's fight. She wouldn't be wanting anyone else to be taking it on for her.

"You've told me nothing. He was here and he was killed here. You are going to tell me why and you are going to tell me who."

"I've told you everything I know," Millie said. "I don't know why and I don't know who."

"And you're lying. I don't believe you."

"Believe what you like. It will make no difference to me. I've asked you to go. If you won't go, you can at least lower your voice."

"I don't intend to lower my voice. I don't care who hears me. I want the whole world to know. My husband was here. He was killed here. You're not going to put it on me."

"I'm not going to put it on anybody," Millie said.

In response to that Marian Douglas did lower her voice. She was shifting into something that I guessed she was less eager to have the whole world hear.

"I'm not pretending that I've suffered any great loss," she said, "or even that I give a damn. So he's dead. It's as good a way of being rid of him as any. I hated him. He was despicable. It's not as though I've lost anything. I was through with him anyhow. I've been saved the trouble of divorcing him, not that I would have minded too much. I could have rather enjoyed spreading the filth over the spotless Mildred Dalton."

"Do you think it's a good idea to be talking like that?" Millie asked. "You hated him. You've been spared the trouble of divorcing him. Have you thought of the way that sounds?"

"That's what I mean—putting it on me. Everybody knows how I felt about him. It's been no secret, so now you think it will be easy to put it on me. You are going to have another think coming."

"You said it. I didn't," Millie said. "All this nonsense about putting it on somebody. Could you be thinking of putting it on me?"

"I'm thinking about that old man. He hated Crate. He wanted to be rid of him. Ever since you started jumping into bed with my husband, that old man wanted nothing more."

"That old man is dying," Millie said. "That old man is too weak and too sick to hurt a fly."

I'd had enough.

"Miss Dalton asked you to leave," I said. "Now I'm telling you. Get out, lady, and don't ever come back."

"Because I can be murdered as well?" She turned away from me and back to Millie. "What about him?" she said, indicating me with a flip of her hand. "He was here. He was down on the beach with Crate. He was the last person to see Crate alive. The last person to see the murdered man alive, isn't that the murderer?"

"You're in no danger of being murdered, Mrs. Douglas," I said. "You are in danger of being thrown out of here."

"You just try it," she said.

I made a move toward her. The rules say you don't manhandle a woman, but there are women and women and times when it has to be that all rules are off. Millie laid a hand on my arm.

"Don't," she said. She turned back to the woman. "If we are going to deal in wild accusations," she said, "you better face it. You're the one who's saying you wanted to be rid of him. Nobody else is saying that."

Mrs. Douglas laughed.

"I'm the one who wasn't over here the night he was killed," she said.

"So you say," Millie said.

"I'm not a liar."

"Am I to take your word for that when you refuse to take mine?" Millie asked.

Dexter chose that moment to come walking in on us. He was stowing his comb as he came through the door. Obviously he had combed his hair in preparation for making his entrance.

"She was nowhere near here," Dexter said. "She was over in her own house. I know. I was with her there. We was in bed."

The lady glared at him.

"There's no need to be so explicit," she said.

"It's nothing to be ashamed of," Dexter said.

He could have been suggesting that it was something in which she should have taken pride. So far as he was concerned, he was boasting of it.

"I'm not ashamed, but there's no need for defending myself. Against them there is certainly no need."

Millie took that with one of those honeyed smiles.

"So you see now," she said. "There's no reason why you shouldn't go. After all, you have an alibi. Nobody can put anything on you, possibly not even a nightgown. Shan't we just leave it that way? You have an alibi and, since I wasn't in bed with anybody, I haven't."

"So pure," the widow woman said.

Dexter snickered. If ever a punk was looking for a thick lip, this had to be it; but Millie had a hold on my arm and she was holding on tight. I would have had to pry her loose and I wasn't about to do that, more than ever not before that audience. She had her own way of handling it. She shot Dexter a look that should have curled his well-combed hair.

"You should be with your patient," she said, "but since you are not, we shall go and sit with him while you see your friend out, and I mean out. If she'll walk, that will be all right. If she must be carried, you can carry her. You know that Dr. Buller wants quiet for his patient. That makes it your job to take care of it."

Keeping her tight hold on my arm, she steered us out of there and down the hall to Sam's room. She wasn't showing it, but I could feel it in the grasp she had on me. She was shaking. I could see what Jerry Buller meant by what he'd said about the good-soldier jazz. I was half wishing that we were going to go in on Sam and find him conscious. It wasn't that I would have wanted him to have heard any of that, but with my ears still throbbing from the screech of the Dalton dame's sound level, I couldn't help thinking that if even that hadn't roused him, nothing ever would again. Of course, Jerry Buller had told me as much, but this was a demonstration and it was painful.

"You didn't need that," I said. "Try to forget it."

"The woman's insane," Millie said.

"The woman's the pluperfect bitch."

"Much the same thing," Millie said. "That's one of the things insanity is, being the pluperfect anything."

So then Dexter came popping his head in the door and damned if he wasn't combing his hair again.

"I turn the general every twenty minutes," he said. "I'm due to turn him now."

He seemed to be asking permission to come into the room.

Millie gave it.

"Yes, of course," she said. "Come and do whatever he needs."

Dexter came into the room and again I was thinking back to something Jerry Buller had said. The guy was the world's premier pain in the ass but he was great at his job. I watched him lift Sam and turn him. It was like what a great pianist does when he goes pianissimo. It's the trick of using the greatest strength to be the most gentle. The ape had to spoil it, of course, by opening his big mouth.

"He won't be needing anything now for the next twenty minutes," he said. "I'd like to run Marian home. I'll be back in plenty of time."

"You'd have to make it a quickie, and not stop to comb your hair," I said.

Millie glowered at me.

"If there's no other way of getting your friend out of here," she said, "go, by all means, but take her car. I don't want it left in the driveway. That means you'll have to run all the way back, but that can't be helped."

"I'll be back for the next time he needs turning."

"You will," Millie said, "or you will have to answer to Dr. Buller."

He made it back on the dot, but he had to answer to Jerry anyhow. He hadn't been forced to run all the way back and he had been on time only because he had picked up a lift. It was Jerry who gave it to him and it didn't suit Jerry at all that he had a nurse on the case who was taking every opportunity to leave the sickroom. It made no difference that he was popping back at the stated intervals at which his patient's position had to be changed. It was also his job to be standing by.

Dexter had a ready argument.

"Nobody can do twenty-four-hour duty," he said. "You can't do it without you take a little break every chance you get. It's not like neglecting the patient."

Buller accepted that, but he told the oaf that it wasn't going to be twenty-four-hour duty.

"Now that the general is in coma," he said, "he needs round-the-clock nursing. So now you're working an eight-hour tour and you won't be taking all these little breaks. I have someone coming in this afternoon at four and another nurse will come on at midnight. You'll stay on for the eight-to-four shift."

Instead of welcoming it, Dexter did an about-face.

"You don't need those other people," he said. "I can handle it."

"Nobody can handle it alone," the doctor said, "not the way I will expect it to be handled."

"It's not the way I work," Dexter said. "You work in shifts with them others and all you got is the messes they leave you to clean up."

Buller shrugged.

"If you don't want it, you don't want it," he said. "I'll expect you to work this shift. I'll line up someone else for tomorrow morning."

"If an eight-hour shift pays less than what you've been getting," Millie said, "it won't. You're not being cut in pay."

"And you'll be having your nights free, man," Buller said. "Don't tell me you don't like your nights."

"I'm human," Dexter said.

"Do your best to be," Buller said. "I'd like to see you try."

For the doctor this had been an unplanned visit. He'd had it in mind to come over after lunch. Coming on Dexter loose in the town when he had expected the man would be with his patient had bothered him, and he had nipped over for a look at Sam. Now he was taking off to grab himself some lunch. He would be back to tell me where I was to go and how I was to get there. Millie had other ideas.

"You'll stay and have lunch with Matt and me," she said.

"I had breakfast here," Buller said. "If I ever found a patient eating that much in one meal, I'd put him on six hundred calories a day for a month. How much can I freeload on you?"

"Much more than I've ever been able to persuade you to try," Millie said.

She went off to ask Clara to set the additional place.

"I suppose there's no harm in Millie knowing where you'll be going," Buller said. "By the way, for your information, the autopsy is being done at the hospital. No full report yet, but the pathologist told me this much. There's no chance it was suicide. Crate Douglas was murdered. He was dead before he went into the water."

"I have a hunch that even now his widow is passing the word that I killed him, acting for Sam," I said.

"That one, she passes a lot of words."

"She was here when I came back. She was demanding that Millie tell her who killed him and why."

"Marian Douglas is poison. She always has been."

"She's not going to let anyone put her husband's murder onto her," I said. "She has an alibi for that night. She was home having it on with Dexter."

"Common knowledge," Buller said. "It's been the big parade. Dexter just happens to be the one who's passing the reviewing stand at the moment."

"I suppose all the others saluted," I said. "Dexter must have combed his hair."

Buller sighed.

"Dexter must have something that you and I can't see," he said. "Even Millie finds him attractive."

"Who says?"

"She told me."

I laughed.

"And you believed her? Oh, Doctor, Doctor."

"Why would she say it if not?"

"To get a rise out of you. You're supposed to be good at reading symptoms. Don't you recognize the symptoms when a girl is courting you?"

"Don't be ridiculous. Millie?"

"Don't be ridiculous. Yes, Millie."

She called us to lunch. The summons put a period to that line of talk.

"Have you told Jerry about my visitor?" she asked.

"I told him."

"A condolence call in reverse," Millie said. "In every way reverse."

"Tell me something, Millie," Buller said. "In all the times you'd been seeing him, did you ever have the idea that Crate Douglas might have been drugging?"

"Crate? Not so I could tell, but you can't always know, can you? It would be different for you, Jerry. I suppose you could—all sorts of little medical things you would notice, but me? I wouldn't know. I've been to parties where people were passing a joint around and I've known some people who take cocaine. I've seen them take it. Some of them do show some sort of effect, but I know people who show nothing at all. At least to my untutored eye they don't. So, if Crate was doing it, he was one of those."

"Why do you ask?" I put the question.

"Since the one person who is known to have hated him

has an alibi," Buller said, "what remains but that he was involved in the marijuana smuggling and he got in over his head with people who were too tough for a half-wit like Crate Douglas? So he came out dead."

"For all her yelling around how she hated him," Millie said, "she never tried to divorce him or anything like that. She needed him."

"What would anybody have needed him for?"

I looked at Millie. She was suppressing a twinkle, but I could detect a trace of something that had to be a smirk of satisfaction. She had struck a spark of retroactive jealousy.

"Not necessarily him," she said, "but a husband and it would have needed to be one like Crate. He was no obstacle to her having lovers and, at the same time, he was her protection against them. She was married. She had a husband. Her other men had to keep their demands within limits. You'll see how fast she's going to dump Dexter now. He was all right as long as there was no possibility that he could get serious."

"It doesn't have to be that he was involved in the smuggling," I said. "Bean walked in on them and he got shot. That doesn't say Bean was involved in the smuggling operation. Why not the same for Douglas?"

"Then why not for you? Nobody hit you on the head."

I shrugged.

"I don't know," I said. "Probably nothing more than the difference between lucky timing and unlucky timing. I could wish his wife didn't have an alibi."

"Why?" Millie asked.

"Murder is her style," I said. "I don't like it for a bunch of stupid kids."

"They didn't kill anyone."

Millie and the doctor spoke together.

"But it happened while a crime was being committed, a crime in which they were involved."

It was the wrong thing to say. It wasn't only that they didn't want to believe it. It made Dr. Jerry Buller almost change his mind about telling me where I could go to find the kids.

"You're prejudging them," he said. "I thought you'd be going to them with an open mind."

"Not permanently closed," I said. "Just temporarily— let's say for repairs. There's one thing they have to know, and there is only the one way they can know it and that is by hearing it from me. It's obvious that they are hiding out only because they think I am bringing charges against them for assault and for siphoning my gas. They're in a bad spot, and by hiding out they are making it worse for themselves. They have to be convinced that I am not bringing charges and that there is nothing that will persuade me to bring charges."

"That's on the assumption that they are innocent of everything else," Buller said. "Since you aren't making that assumption, you can't really be thinking that it's only because of what you might do that they have taken off."

"Yes, I can," I said. "They were on the beach. They were unloading the marijuana. When Bean came in on them, they pulled it off the beach and took it back to the boat. When I heard splashes out on the bay, I thought they were the sound of people diving into the water. I thought skinny-dipping even though it seemed unbelievably silly. Of course, I was wrong. Those splashes were something else. They were made by the weighted bales hitting the water. But Bean was dead and they were into something bigger than they had anticipated, something too big for them. That finished it for them.

They pulled out on the smuggling deal. That's why they weren't back on the water to haul the bales in when the stuff came up to the surface."

Millie caught the significance of what I was saying.

"It makes sense, Jerry," she said. "They didn't take off yesterday. They were around all day. They thought they were all right because they hadn't been caught red-handed. It may have been stupid of them to think that, but we know they're stupid. Last night caught them red-handed and that was different. That made them run. It makes sense. They hadn't run away from their big problem."

"That's it," I said. "They aren't thinking in terms of the relative magnitude of the crimes. They are thinking only in terms of the relative likelihood of being caught or of having anything proven against them. They're thinking they can hide out until their difficulty with me will have blown over, and they are right about that."

Buller picked it up.

"But they can't hide out forever," he said. "Not long enough for marijuana and two murders to blow over. So you want to tell them that they have nothing to fear from you but plenty to fear from murder charges."

"Exactly," I said, "and I want to try to make them understand that by running from a danger that doesn't exist, they are setting up presumptions that are making the bad spot they are in immeasurably worse. They need to be out in the open where their friends can help them work at clearing themselves of the murders."

Millie moaned.

"But you just said that the murders came in connection with a crime they were committing and that puts them in it regardless of whether they did the killings or not," she said.

"Yes," I said. "They have to be made to understand that. It's no good their thinking they're not in trouble and it's no good anyone trying to tell them they are not. They have to understand the exact nature of the spot they're in and that their only hope will lie in the clemency they might expect as young offenders but then only if they can convince people—prosecutor, judge, jury, the folks here in town—that their guilt is limited. They didn't shoot Bean. They didn't murder Douglas."

"Who did?" Millie asked.

"The kids know the answer to that question," I said. "It's hardly possible that they wouldn't know, and that opens up further hope for them. They can talk. They can cooperate with the law."

CHAPTER 9

I had Millie with me and between us we wore Buller down. He told me where I'd find the hideout and how I could get there. He'd brought a road map with him and he had marked the roads for me.

"It's an old fishing and hunting camp," he said. "It's deep in the woods and it's been abandoned and falling into ruin for at least fifty years. I would guess that it may have been sixty years and more. It should have been gone long since and the road through the woods should have been overgrown and obliterated. The only reason why there may be anything left of either the camp or the road is because of what I told you. Generation after generation, kids have been using it and, generation after generation, they've made stabs at patching it up and at keeping the track more or less open. Even in my time it wasn't anything much more than shelter of sorts and just about barely accessible. By now it will be even more broken down and more overgrown, but you can get in there."

"Can my car make it?" I asked.

"In my day you could get a car all the way in," Buller said. "I'd be surprised if you still could, but you won't want to anyway. If you drove all the way in, they'd know you were coming long before you could get there and you'd find the place empty. They'd be off in the woods where you'd never catch up with them."

We had moved it into the sickroom where Buller and I were giving Dexter his break for lunch. Clara always took off for a couple of hours in the afternoon. She had served us and had left lunch for Dexter. Millie was serving it up to him and then was going to nip up the road to look in on Martha Ainsley confined to her bed. She had promised to bring Martha a book.

Buller told me how to find the track into the woods and where he thought I could best leave the track. He gave me a detailed description of the terrain, and he drew me a little map I could follow for circling around to come on the camp ruin from a direction that we could expect wouldn't be watched.

When he had given me everything I needed to know, I went to the bedside table. Buller was reading my mind.

"You won't need that," he said.

"I think I will."

"What for?"

"Okay. We both know I can talk the ear off a teacup. I'm a persuasive guy, but I need people who will hold still to listen long enough so that they can even begin to be persuaded. At the point of a gun I can hold them. Otherwise what are my chances?"

"With a gun there's always the possibility of an accident."

"I'm not clumsy with guns. I don't have accidents."

I could see that he didn't like it, but he wasn't saying anything more.

I pulled the drawer open. The .45 wasn't there. I didn't like that, but Buller was divided. It was evident that he was feeling what I was feeling, but along with it he was relieved. It was his preference that I should go into those woods unarmed.

"I put it back," I said. "I put it here. You saw me. So who?"

"Millie," Buller said.

"Or Dexter. There's been no one else but you and me."

"You can't ask him about it now without Millie knowing."

"And if she doesn't know, it's better that she stay ignorant."

"And better that she shouldn't find out that we know," Buller said. "Do you think she could understand?"

"You know she couldn't," I said.

"I know."

I pushed the drawer shut.

"If it's been put back in the desk, I'll take it," I said.

"And if it isn't?"

"I'll take the rifle. The rifle might even be better, more intimidating."

I checked the desk drawer. I checked all the drawers. No .45. I got the rifle out of the gun case and I asked Millie to keep Mathilda. It wasn't the time of year for going into the woods with dog and gun. It was months away from hunting season.

"She'll be fine," Millie said. "She'll be company for me and I'll take her along to Martha's when I go."

Jerry Buller's directions were great. It was no trick at all to follow the roads he'd marked and, going by the landmarks he had given me, I had a fairly easy time of it finding the place where the track to the camp took off into the woods. I'd been having my doubts about how well successive generations of kids could have done at keeping even a track open. As Jerry had indicated it would be, however, it was no more than passable but it was there. This wasn't one of your forests of mixed hardwoods where, without constant clearing, you'll have a tangle of undergrowth taking over. There were pine-woods, and pine carpets the ground with its needles. They tend to hold other growth down.

Following Jerry's instructions, I took Baby in only as far as I had to. Since the track was tortuous, I soon came to a spot where I could leave her and she would be out of sight of the road. Coming up the track on foot, I was able to move fast since the place where Jerry had suggested I leave it for circling around to the surprise angle would be something I couldn't miss. There would be a brook. I was to cross the brook and then leave the trail to follow the stream off to the right. It was to be simple enough. The brook took a wide turn. Following it, I would be coming up on the rear of the camp.

"There used to be a bridge, but even in my time it had been long gone," Jerry had said. "We used to wade the brook. At the trail, where you'll be crossing, it's shallow, never more than a foot deep except in the spring when everything floods. Right now it will be less than a foot. Behind the camp there's a place where it widens into a pool and runs deep. It was a good swimming hole."

I came to the stream and, as Jerry had predicted, the water was low. I shucked out of my shoes and socks and crossed to the far side. That water was colder than you could believe. I visualized a pool where it would run deep and, if anything, be even colder, and I was remembering Jerry's look when he had been speaking of the swimming hole. Wistful would be the only word for it. For the moment, he had been thinking back to his Huck Finn days.

Off the trail the going was less easy, but it was possible all the way and, when you are walking on a layer of pine needles, you don't have to be a character out of

Fenimore Cooper to keep your movements silent. I kept
as close to the stream as I could. I didn't want to risk
straying away from it, and Jerry had given me landmarks
as I would see them from brookside. I couldn't count on
recognizing them if I were to come on them from any
other angle.

I didn't need the landmarks. Before I caught even the
first sight of them, I got lucky. I had something else to
guide on. It was shouting and laughing, hooting and
giggling. It was splashing and it was just up ahead. Talk
about *déjà vu*. It could have taken me back to my own
Huck Finn days if there hadn't been the intrusion of the
fresher memory. These were the voices and such was the
nonsense that I'd heard from the beach at the beginning
of all this.

They were swimming and nothing could have been
better for my purposes. It couldn't be any great, broad
expanse of water. It would only be a small swimming
hole. So now I had them neatly clumped together for
holding them under the menace of the rifle. I would also
have them with their pants off. As jailers and prisoners
know all too well, a naked man under the eye of a man
with his clothes on stands at a great psychological disadvantage.

If I had been moving carefully before this, now I was
stealing along, silent and watchful. As I came up on
them, I shifted away from the water but only just far
enough to put a screen of trees between me and the pool.
Did I say I got lucky? The luck was holding, because
hanging from the branches of my screen of trees were
jeans and shirts. It took only a step or two forward to put
me between them and their clothes.

I stepped forward. Two who had been poised at the
edge of the swimming hole took one look at me and dove

in. Bobbing up to the surface, they dragged in a long breath and went back down under. The ones who had already been in the water also went under. They had no place else to hide. The water was clear and I could see them there, holding themselves down.

It was just to wait the few moments until they would surface. They had no blocks of rock salt to hold them down and in any case they would have to come up for air. They came up.

"I'm here as your friend," I said. "Jerry Buller sent me—Dr. Buller. If you don't know that he's your friend, you should."

They had taken in their air and had submerged again. I wasn't at all certain that they had grasped what I'd been saying. I couldn't even know that they had heard. When you're in swimming, you have to shake the water out of your ears before you'll be hearing well. I waited till they came up again.

"If you don't believe me, just think," I said. "How do you suppose I found you?"

That was all I could get in before they went under again. So again I waited for the next intake of air.

"If it was what I wanted, I could pick you off here and now," I said. "It would be like shooting fish in a barrel."

Not original? Of course not, but was it ever said when it was a better fit to the circumstances? They were starting down again but they changed their minds. My words were getting to them at least to the extent of making them realize that the water was giving them not much in the way of cover and almost nothing in the way of concealment.

"What do you want?" one of them asked.

Now that they were all on the surface and stationary, I could take a count. I had the lot, all five of them. The one who had spoken was the kid I had slapped. I gave them their orders. There was a good stretch of smooth flat rock at the edge of the pool. I told them to climb out of the water and settle in a bunch on the rock where the sun would warm them and dry them.

"You'll climb up there and you'll stay there," I said. "I'm going to talk and you're going to listen. That's all. There are things you need to know and those are the things I've come to tell you. That and nothing else. I talk. You listen. After that it will be up to you. I'll go away and leave you. It will be up to you to make your own decisions, whether you'll begin to get smart or you'll go on as you are doing and hang yourselves."

They exchanged glances and I knew what they were thinking. They were expecting me to feed them all the old stuff they had heard too many times before, middle-aged exhortations to mend their ways. Think what they would, however, they were under the gun. They did as they were told but not, of course, without grumbling. Fresh out of the water, they looked a more savory crew than they had been. They were glisteningly clean.

"We ain't done nothing," they said, more or less in chorus.

"You settle down and listen," I said. "I'll tell you what you done. But roll call first. Your names."

"Slocum."

"Amos."

Those were the post office pair. Orville had been on the nose in his identifications—Slo and Quick.

"Hobart."

"Clemson."

"Joshua."

"First, why you are hiding out here? Last night I caught you siphoning gas out of my car. It was that and it was assault, and you know that, if I should want to bring charges, I can make them stick and you would be for it. You also know that I'm not going to be around here long, so you've been thinking that you need only to hide out until I go away and then you can go home and you'll be okay. I came to tell you that you are wrong. You're wrong two ways. You don't have to hide out because of last night. I haven't brought charges and I'm not going to. You didn't get enough gas to talk about and the assault—I started it in the post office."

I said nothing about the obvious difference between a man-to-man, one-on-one encounter and a gang attack, but I had more important things to ram into their thick heads. I wasn't there to improve their manners or even to give them lessons in sportsmanship.

"What are you going to do?" Slo asked.

He could have been thinking that I had come to shoot them.

"Nothing. Just what I am doing now. I'm going to tell you what you need to know and then I'm going away. So here's the rest of it. You're in trouble, bad trouble, and it has nothing to do with me."

"Then why don't you just mind your own business, mister?" Quick asked.

Slo turned on him.

"Shut up and listen to the man," he said. "It ain't going to hurt none to listen."

"Who's he to tell us?"

"He's the man with the gun, stupid."

"Believe it or not," I said, "I'm your friend. Dr. Buller is your friend, and any friends of Jerry Buller's are friends of mine. Also you are you. You're stupid. You're in over your head, and you need all the friends you can get. You were on the beach night before last, bringing a load of marijuana ashore. That's smuggling and that's in violation of the narcotics laws. You didn't succeed in bringing it in, so maybe it's only attempted violation and conspiracy to violate, but that's more than enough. More than that, though, there's worse. There's also murder. So the State Troopers are looking for killers and, just when they were fresh out of suspects, you guys take off and go into hiding. You know and I know why you're doing it, but that's not the way the troopers and most other people are seeing it. They think you're telling them that you are killers."

"We didn't shoot Beebee," Slo said. "We didn't even know it was marijuana. If we knowed it was mari'uana, we wouldn't ever have worked so cheap."

"What did you think it was?"

"We didn't know. He didn't tell us. He didn't even tell us it was smuggling."

"Come on! Unloading in the dark from a boat without riding lights?"

"He said it had to be a secret. It was a surprise for his wife."

"I can just believe that. It seems to me you guys are stupid enough to have believed it."

"What's stupid? He has a wife. They're rich."

I knew what was coming and it was like a kick in the gut.

"Who?" I asked, praying for an answer that might prove me wrong.

"Crate Douglas, that's who."

I could hear Trooper Boudreau as he would react to that. Putting it onto a dead man—it was going to sound too convenient. I said nothing about that. I wanted to explore and to learn, if I could, whether or not they knew that Douglas was dead along with Bean.

"Tell me exactly what happened," I said. "All of it from the beginning."

They couldn't have been more lacking in the skill and the orderliness of mind it takes to give a coherent and consecutive account of events. They backed and filled. They wandered off into irrelevancies. Again and again I had to stop them and nudge them back on the track, but I got their story out of them and to me it had the ring of truth. I couldn't believe that, even putting their five heads together, this quintet of young dolts could have accumulated a pool of wit sufficient for concocting a lie that was so precise a fit to every point of the evidence.

Creighton Douglas had hired them and they had worked cheap. Ten dollars for each of them. They had gone out with him in his boat in the afternoon and it had been a ball, just lying around on the deck and drinking beer while he had the boat skylarking around all over the place.

They had gone out among the other pleasure boats, running down past Belfast and then back up Bar Harbor way. It was fun. It was living the way the rich kids lived, and they were even being paid for it. They would have done it for nothing. I could have told them that they had done it for nothing. I was wondering whether Douglas had been that cheap or if the low rate of pay had been one of his ways of snowing the kids into thinking that what he was involving them in was no big deal.

I kept those speculations to myself. I wanted their story. I wasn't throwing in anything that could confuse them.

Toward the end of the afternoon, Douglas pulled away from the other pleasure craft and headed out to sea. Well out from shore they met another boat. They described it as another beautiful job like the Douglas boat but bigger, more like a yacht. Five small waterproof bales with attached weights and long lines were loaded into Douglas' boat and they ran back toward shore. I made a mental note of the number. Only four had come up. The lobstermen had hauled four in.

At the mouth of the bay Douglas left them, taking off in one of the boat's two dinghies. He told them to play around outside. He told them to have fun. There were steaks and fixings in the galley. They were to help themselves to anything they wanted.

Their instructions were to stay out until three in the morning and then to come back in without lights and to anchor off the backshore. I had to ask them whether that hadn't made them think. They said it had, but it was his boat and, if he wanted to take his chances on getting it wrecked, why should they care?

"It was crazy, sure," Joshua said, "but all that beer. We was all drunk by then. Nothing looked crazy, not then."

They were to be off the backshore at four o'clock. Using the dinghy that was still with them, they were to put the bales ashore. Douglas would meet them on the beach to load the bales into his car, and that would be it. They'd only have to run the boat around the point and moor it at the Douglas boathouse. Then they could take off.

"We was putting the stuff on the beach and we was having fun. Full of beer and all, we was horsing around. Douglas came and told us to hold it down and it was right then that Beebee came. Douglas didn't wait for nothing. He shot Beebee."

Even full of beer, of course, they panicked at that, but Douglas told them it was his thing and he wasn't going to let them be involved in it. They were to get away from there and fast, and they were to get rid of the bales. That

way they would be out of it. They were to haul the stuff
back to the boat and out there they were to dump it into
the bay. He told them it was weighted and it would sink.
Nobody would ever know about it. They'd have the boat
for their quick getaway. If they ran it around to the
Douglas boat landing as planned, they would be out of it.
They had nothing to worry about.

"Didn't he tell you that the bales were weighted to stay
down only about twenty-four hours and that they'd be
coming back to the surface for you to haul them in the
next night?" I asked.

"That's nuts."

They were all talking at once now. Weights were
weights. You throw them into the water and they go
down and stay down. They don't come up unless you
haul them up.

"Those weights were salt," I told them. "The marijuana
was in watertight bales, but the blocks of salt were in or-
dinary canvas sacks. The salt dissolves in the water and
the bales come back up. They came up this morning. The
Coast Guard has them."

They groaned in unison. Slo was the only one who
spoke.

"That old bastard, Crate Douglas," he said. "We got to
fix him. He suckered us. He was suckering us all the
way."

They could call him Slo, but of the lot of them he
seemed to have the quickest mind. Nobody could call it
lightning fast, but, compared to the others, he was far out
ahead.

"After that," I said, "you did as Douglas told you. You
left him there on the beach. You took the bales back out
to the boat and you dumped them. Then you ran the boat

back to his boat landing. When was the next time you saw him?"

They hadn't seen him again. They explained that they'd made a point of not seeing him again. He had killed Bean. They had seen him do it and that had been too much. They weren't going to have any part of him after that. Fun is fun, but not when it got you mixed up with a killer. That much good sense they did have.

"He was going to be mad at us anyway," Hobie said.

"Because you loused the deal up with your noise?" I said. "He was the one who fed you the beer. He got you drunk."

"It wasn't that," Hobie said.

He went on to tell me what it was. In hauling the bales off the beach, they had somehow missed out on one of the five. Back out on the bay, when they were ditching them in the water, they found themselves one short on the count. They had considered going back in to pick it up, but Douglas had told them to take off and, after all, they had left him on the beach with the dead cop. They couldn't but have been thinking that they would be better away from there.

"One bale complete with its weights?" I asked.

"Not all of it," Hobie said. "I had the iron weight and the line. I was hauling it along by that. Somehow the rest of it broke loose and I didn't notice. It was the bale and the bag that was lashed to it. You say that was salt. All that part was what I lost."

"You're sure that's the way you lost it?"

"Of course, I'm sure. There was the five of the things and the five of us guys. We was each taking one. Mine come loose."

"It wasn't wasted," I said. "Douglas was knocked on

the head and the salt weight was tied on to him to sink
his body in the bay. The body came up with the marijuana. The tide washed him ashore this morning."

That piece of news knocked the five of them over.

"So that's where you stand," I said. "It's two murders
and you guys are being hunted for both of them. It's no
good your running because there's no place you can run.
It's not only the troopers after you for murder. It's also
the Feds for the narcotics deal. I'm not going to try telling you that you can get out of this without paying a
price, but the way you're going, you're making it too expensive. When you're caught—and you will be caught—
they'll throw the book at you. Make no mistake about
that."

"But we didn't kill nobody. They got to believe we
didn't."

"The way you're doing it, you're making them believe
you did kill. You come in and tell your whole story. You
cooperate with the law, like telling the Coast Guard everything you know about the boat Douglas met outside,
and you'll pick yourself up a helluva lot of clemency.
Work hard at cooperating on the marijuana deal and
clear yourselves of the murder charges. You'll have help.
Not everybody will be against you. You can count on me,
on Dr. Buller, and on Mrs. Ainsley. There's also General
Dalton's granddaughter. She's on your side, too. You'll
have people with you and they are people who pull a lot
of weight. You better believe me. It's your best chance.
No. It's your only chance."

They were looking to each other. No one of them
seemed able to decide on his own. Each seemed to be
waiting for one of the others to take the lead. Slo was the
one who broke out of it. He was shaping up to be the
brightest of the lot.

"We come in," he said. "We'll get grabbed before we can tell anybody we was coming in to cooperate. Once they've grabbed us, they'll never believe we was going to give ourselves up."

"You could get your pants on and come in with me," I said.

That brought me a concerted murmur of rejection. They thought I was trying to stampede them. They weren't going to be brought in, not by Erridge or anyone else. Slo broke out of it, holding the lead.

"We'll think about it," he said. "If we come in, it'll be tonight after dark when we can get to my house and nobody see us. We'll get there and we'll telephone the troopers. We'll tell them we're there and we want to come in and cooperate. We'll do it that way."

He had begun that with reservations. It was only something they might decide to do, but even while he was talking, just through the process of lining up ways and means, I could see that he was convincing himself. By the time he had finished, he was talking about something he intended to do. He had done his thinking about it.

The way out to where I'd left Baby was easier than the way I'd taken coming in. Now I did the whole route by the trail. The kids came with me as far as the brook and they brought out planks they had hidden away in the woods so I could go across on those. I didn't have to wade the stream. They had the planks, of course, so that they could cross the stream on their motorcycles.

All the way back to town I was thinking about what I had done. It came to me that in the process of trying to convince the kids, I had been doing something more. I had also been working at convincing myself. I believed their version of what they had done and not done. About their account of what they had known and not known I did have some reservations. It could well have been that they were less innocent than they were pretending and that they had known what the five little bales contained or that they had at least had some suspicion of it.

I knew enough of local history to guess that in all probability at least some of the five might have grandfathers who told glowing tales of their own teenage years—the Prohibition years when in the dark of the night they had gone out to the ships that lay offshore and picked up the cases of whiskey for the local bootleggers.

I could well imagine that for these lads there might have been something of a tradition for acting in defiance of an unpopular law.

There was only one thing they had told me that gave any measure of credibility to their claim of not having known what they were bringing in. They would certainly have known that their forebears in the hire of bootleggers had been better paid. Even in terms of the more robust dollar of the Prohibition years the going wage would have been far more than a ten-spot.

It was likely that by being niggardly Douglas had cheated them in two ways, cheated them of a pay that would have been commensurate with the risk they were taking and cheated them as well out of any understanding of the dimensions of that risk. I had as good as told them that if they came in and cooperated, they could clear themselves of the suspicion of murder and that they would be up against no more than the narcotics charges.

Alone now, behind Baby's steering wheel, I was less certain. I did believe them, but now I was looking at the tacit promise I had left with them, that Millie and Jerry and Martha would also believe them. I felt confident that I wasn't off-base there, but there was Trooper Steve Boudreau. There would be the prosecuting attorney's

office. Was I so certain that they would accept this story
the kids were telling? If they didn't accept it, there could
be a murder trial. It could still be that they would be
confronting a hanging judge and a lynch-minded jury.

I had promised them help. I would help them and
Millie and Jerry and Martha. What could that help
amount to? We could get them a good lawyer. We could
pay for their defense. We could go all the way, financing
appeals. I couldn't convince myself that it would necessarily come to enough. Even with all this revisionary
thinking, I couldn't regret what I had done. I could only
be less happy about it. I hadn't lied to them. What I had
urged on them would be their best chance, but with
every mile I covered on the road back to town, more and
more it was coming to seem too short of being good
enough.

There was only one thing that could with any certainty
bring them out from under the threat of a murder trial.
So there was a question. It was a big question and mile
after mile it grew to where it was taking over the whole
of my thinking.

We knew who shot Beebee Bean, but there was still a
killer to be found: Creighton Douglas' killer. There was
one item in the story the boys had given me that was
going to stand damningly against them. They hadn't
known that the weights used to take the bales down had
been soluble. It was obvious that the killer had operated
under exactly such ignorance. The killer had thought that
the body, sent to the bottom of the bay, would remain
down there anchored by the weight.

The killer had to be found and the killer's guilt established beyond any possibility of doubt, and who was
there to take that on if it wasn't Matt Erridge? Not Millie
certainly and not Martha Ainsley. Not even Dr. Jerry

Buller. He had Sam to watch over. He had his other patients. Lives rested in his hands and they took precedence over the lives that were gone. They would even have to take precedence over the jeopardy in which the five young idiots were standing.

I was elected. If you like, I was electing myself. There was the one obvious place to start and that would be with the dead man's wife. It was common knowledge that there had been not much between them but hate. Hating him, she had, nevertheless, through some twisted motive hung on to him. Her hold on him had been her money, but the time had come when that hold wasn't going to remain effective.

True enough, any hope Douglas had been nurturing of making a switch to Millie had been dashed, but his wife couldn't have known that. There had been no time for her to learn it. Also he had developed another string to his bow. He was going to have money of his own. Setting himself up in the tea trade, he'd been making his bid for something fat in the way of financial independence.

The lady had the motive and the lady had the muscle, but the lady also had an alibi. I was looking at that alibi. She had been in great haste to establish it. What other reason would she have had for coming to the house and making that ridiculous scene if it hadn't been to give Dexter the opening for blurting out her alibi? That the nature of the alibi was such that for many women it would have been embarrassing to let it be known I was discounting. If there was one thing I knew about Marian Douglas, it was that modest reticence wasn't her style.

Asking myself how good her alibi might be, I rated it as anything but strong. There was nothing about that twerp, Dexter, to suggest that he couldn't have been bought. I had been a witness to the moment when he had come forward with her alibi. It had obviously been a service he had enjoyed performing. For a guy like Dexter, the pleasure of sexual boasting had been a delightful fringe.

I had taken on the job and by the time I was back in town I had a good idea of what was going to be involved in doing the job. The lady had to be stripped of her alibi. How I was going to go about doing that I had no idea. All I knew was that I had to give it my best try. I headed for the house, Sam's house, not hers.

I still had to work out ways and means. Also I had been away for hours, and this other thing would have to wait if it should be that Millie or Jerry Buller needed me for anything. There was also the matter of reporting to Jerry that I had seen the kids and how things were standing with them. I had, after all, gone out to the camp in the woods as Jerry's deputy.

Back at the house, however, all that went out of my mind—not all the way out, of course, but it withdrew to something like a waiting area. Millie and Jerry were with Sam. Dexter wasn't around. The woman who was taking the four-to-midnight tour had relieved him.

There was a shocking change in Sam. Except for his thready breathing, he had been motionless, inert. Now he was in motion with a violent facial twitching. Millie grabbed at my hand and hung on. I took her in my arms and tried to turn her away from watching. She fought that off, but she did go on clinging to me.

"Renal failure," Jerry said. "It's agonizing to watch, but it isn't agonizing for him. I can promise you that. He doesn't know."

He was only in part talking to me. It was what he had been telling Millie and he had to keep repeating it for her.

"It will stop soon," he said, "and after it stops, he will go. It will be quiet and peaceful, just fading out."

"I know," Millie said. "I'm ready to accept it. I have been ready for a long time and I can even be happy for him. I did my grieving at the beginning of all this, when he first lost the independence of doing for himself. It was then that he died."

It was what I had been about to say to her. She was saying it for herself and for me.

"Nobody could have known General Sam without knowing that," Jerry said.

"It's wonderful that he's had you for a doctor," Millie said. "I know how much you put into keeping his dignity for him."

"Love and respect," Jerry said. "I wish I could have done more."

We stood the watch and it went just as Jerry had called it. It was almost twenty minutes before the twitching stopped. After that it could have been a deep sleep but only for about a half hour. That was the end.

The first day I was there he had given me an envelope. I went to my room and opened it. It was the instructions for his funeral, complete, concise, and efficiently organized in all detail. It might have been an order of battle.

I got on the phone and made the necessary calls. Before I had finished, Martha Ainsley arrived. She had been watching the road and, when she had seen the nurse drive out hours before her shift would have ended, Martha had known.

"I've been in bed long enough," she said. "I don't want a word out of you, Jerry Buller. Tomorrow I may do as you tell me, but tonight I shall be here with Millie. You might know what is good for me, but right now I'm the one who knows better."

Jerry gave her no argument.

"Thank you for coming," he said.

It was Millie who was the first to bring us back to the living. She asked the question.

"Did you find the boys, Matt?" she asked.

I gave them the full rundown on it.

"He's dead and all that," Millie said, "and he died horribly. I suppose I shouldn't be saying it, but I came to recognize that he was the stinker Sam always said he was, but I don't think even Sam could have guessed how much a stinker."

"Do you think they will do it?" Martha asked. "Will they come in tonight and give themselves up?"

"I think they will," I said, "but I've come around to wondering how much good it can do them."

I filled them in on the thinking I'd been doing on the drive back into town. Jerry was skeptical. It wasn't that he had a high opinion of Marian Douglas. He just couldn't go for the motive.

"She could have divorced him," he said. "She would probably have had to buy him off but that would only have been money. There's never been much good I could say for her, but there is that. She isn't stingy."

Millie and Martha took a tougher view.

"You're a bright boy," Martha said, "but there is one area where you're not bright. You don't know women."

"She couldn't stand it that he should leave her," Millie said. "She has a nasty temper and she has her own kind of pride. Men don't finish with Marian Douglas. She's the one who calls the turn. It has to be that she is through with them. She kicks them out."

"Exactly," Martha said. "With lovers it has always been easy. You can kick a lover out. A husband is more difficult."

"It's been a long time since divorce was difficult," Jerry said.

"I don't know about that," Martha said. "For her? With her reputation, all the affairs she's had and the way she's paraded them?"

I moved.

"I'm going to go and talk to her," I said.

"Condolence call?" Millie asked.

"Throw some ideas at her and watch for a reaction," I said.

"Watch yourself," Martha said. "Around here there's always a rock handy."

"I go forewarned," I said, and I went.

The house was across the town on the other shore of the neck. It was bigger than Sam's or Martha's but not more attractive, just more ostentatious. It wasn't in the class of the monumental jobs they used to call "Maine cottages," but it was somewhere in between. Perhaps I should have taken a look in the garage before I went into the house, but it would have made no difference even if I had seen Dexter's Volks.

I did go down to the boat landing to board the boat for a look around. She was a beautiful job and she had been manned by pigs. The galley was deep in dirty dishes and strewn garbage. There were empty beer cans all over the place and no guess on how many more may have gone over the side. Everything testified to the way the kids had told it. They had been given the run of the boat and they'd had a ball. Of course, they hadn't cleaned up after themselves and nobody else had done it either.

I went up the slope to the house. There was no bell on the front door. I banged the knocker. Dexter came and opened the door. For once he wasn't with the comb in his hand. Her lusty bellow came at us from somewhere in the house.

"Now that you're at the door," she said, "keep going and don't come back."

Dexter stood in the doorway.

"What do you want?" he asked.

"To see Mrs. Douglas. I'd like to talk to her."

"This wouldn't be the time for it. She's in a temper. You heard her."

"Was that for me or for you?" I asked.

The lady appeared behind him. She addressed herself to me.

"Once you're here," she said, "you can do me a favor and throw this son-of-a-bitch out."

I hadn't come there to do her any favors, but she was asking something of me that was close to irresistible. Dexter stepped back from the door. He wasn't moving out of my reach. He was just indicating that he was there to stay. He brought out his comb and started working on his hair. His hair didn't need it. It wasn't ruffled. I don't know whether it was force of habit or his way of showing that he was also unruffled.

"The lady wants you to go," I said.

"See now?" she said. "The man catches on quick. What makes you so slow?"

"Because I know you better than you know yourself," Dexter said. "I know you need me, and when you calm down, you'll know it, too."

I couldn't have hoped for better. It had to be that he was reminding her of the alibi he had given her.

"Get out," she said.

"You'll be sorry."

"I don't need you and I don't need you to lie for me."

"You'll regret this," Dexter said.

"Get out and stay out."

I stepped aside to give him room to pass. She took a step toward him, and he retreated. For all his size and strength, he seemed to be afraid of her. I was telling myself that I could understand that. Any man would tread warily if he was mixed up with a dame who had knocked her husband's head in with a rock and was now enraged with him.

"When you come to your senses, you'll know where to find me," he said, as he pulled out.

She came and stood with me in the doorway while we watched him go to the garage and come back out at the wheel of his Volks. She watched the car till it had turned into the street and had moved out of sight. Then she spoke to me. She even smiled.

"Come in," she said. "I'll give you a drink."

Off with the old and on with the new and that quick? It seemed too quick even for this babe. I wasn't taking any drink even though my mouth was dry. There's a dryness that drink won't help.

"What's with him?" I asked.

"He's a clown. He wants me to marry him. He had the nerve to tell me I had to do it. I had no choice."

"Because he lied for you?"

"As though I needed it. The man's ridiculous."

"He wasn't with you that night?"

"Not that late. Not when Crate was killed. It was after four when you saw Crate alive. This ape left here at four."

"Let's go," I said.

"What do you mean 'let's go'? You can come in and have a drink or not. Suit yourself. I'm not going anywhere."

I took a good hold on her arm.

"You're coming with me."

"Where?"

"First we'll have a talk with Dexter and then it will be up to the police."

"Don't be a fool."

"If you prefer, I can call the police right now. They'll come here to get you."

"I don't care what you do. Here or elsewhere, I don't care where you choose to make a fool of yourself."

"I do have a preference," I said. "I shouldn't have. let Dexter go. Boudreau will want to talk to him."

"You're determined to make a fool of yourself," she said. "Now I'm going to surprise you. I'll help you. Just for laughs, I'm going with you. I'm ready if you are."

I kept my hold on her arm, but I didn't need it. She had turned flirtatious. She was even giggling. It was no trouble putting her in the Porsche. She jumped in.

I pulled Baby out of the driveway. Going through the town, I let the Porsche do her stuff. Do I have to tell you what Baby's stuff does to speed laws? If Beebee Bean had lived to be in his favorite lurking place by the golf links, he would have pulled me in. If Trooper Boudreau or any of his men had witnessed my passage, they would have done it. I wasn't letting any of that worry me. I had her in the car. If they picked me up, it could have saved me calling them.

We came whizzing into Sam's driveway. As I'd expected, the Volks was there. There was the Douglas house and there was Sam's. In that town, Dexter would have had no other place to go. I spoke to her as we were getting out of the car.

"Is it any good my asking you to behave yourself?" I asked. "General Dalton died only a couple of hours ago."

"So what? He was older than God and even more right-
eous," she said. "I'll try not to laugh."

There wasn't anything I could do with that but let it
pass.

Using my key, I opened the front door and promptly
forgot all about Marian Douglas. The house has a spa-
cious central hall, but, for all its size, it was crowded. Everyone was there. Backed at the far end and facing me,
Millie, Martha, Clara, and Jerry stood in a tight row.
Right in front of them Mathilda was having herself a
great game with a lot of shreds of torn-up plastic. The
floor was strewn with grass.

Almost within my reach and backing toward me was
Dexter. He was brandishing Sam's .45, using it to hold
Jerry and the women off. I jumped him from behind. In
the process of taking him, I was careful to get his gun
hand up. A shot went off. It did the ceiling plaster no
good, but better there than where he had been aiming it.
I wrestled him to the floor. Jerry jumped forward and
wrenched the gun out of the guy's hand. Even while I
was getting him down, the whole thing came clear to me.
It didn't take much doing.

There had been five bales of the grass but only four
had bobbed up to be hauled in by the lobstermen. I knew
from the boys that the fifth, complete with its attached
weight of salt, had been left on the beach. In his ignorance, Creighton Douglas' killer had used that fifth salt
weight for sinking Douglas' body. That left nothing but
the one bale of marijuana unaccounted for, and who
could have had it but Douglas' killer? There had been
Dexter's alibi, but it was the kind of alibi that could work
both ways and, with the lady repudiating it, it wasn't
working at all.

He had been selling Marian Douglas on the idea that,

with the way she had been talking about her husband, she needed an alibi for the time of Creighton Douglas' murder. He had given her one and then, on the strength of it, he had tried to blackmail her into marriage. All the time, of course, he had been giving himself an alibi, but he had misjudged his woman.

He had been on his way back to the house that night, and he had spotted Douglas' car where it was parked by the beach. He had gone down to the beach, stealing along in there to see what he could see. Perhaps he had hoped to find Douglas there with Millie, giving him a chance to go back to the man's wife with something she could use for divorce grounds. Perhaps he had expected he would find Douglas alone. Either way, he did find Douglas alone and standing over Bean's dead body. He thought it a great opportunity. He killed Douglas. The fool had been thinking that all it would be needing could be to get her loose from her husband, and she and her money would be his for the taking.

That had been Dexter's night since it brought him a bonus as well. There was the bale of marijuana with its attached weight. The weight was just what he needed for disposing of the body, or so he thought since he didn't know it was salt. The marijuana would be something he could convert to ready cash for bridging him over to the wedding day.

He had stowed the marijuana somewhere in his room at Sam's. What safer place could there have been for storing his loot than in a house so eminently above suspicion? He had reckoned without Mathilda. Old buddy dog, with everyone in the house preoccupied, had been having a boring time of it. So she had amused herself as best she could. Tearing stuff up and strewing it around, that's good puppy fun and what could it be but the marijuana?

As police in lots of places have discovered, dogs have a nose for it.

And that was it. We called Boudreau and they came and got Dexter. It later came out that he had also been doing a little sideline in uppers and downers. You've got it. Dexter was the one who always emptied Sam's wastebasket.

The kids came in that night. They were booked on the marijuana-smuggling charge. We stood bail for them and they did a good job of cooperating. The last I heard of them, they had drawn suspended sentences and were on probation. Jerry tells me there's a good chance that they'll have grown up by the time their probation period will be over.

Sam's will was something of a shocker. There were generous bequests to the people who had worked for him and mementoes to friends like Martha Ainsley and myself. He left Millie the house and its contents, but the residuary legatee was Gerald Buller, M.D. I got it out of Millie without too much trouble. She and Sam had cooked that one up between them.

"He has to marry me now to save me from want," she said.

I have never seen a more self-satisfied smirk.

Need I tell you that he did? I have a godson now. His name is Sam Buller. Mathilda thinks he's hers.